SPELLS, WISHES & DREAMS

SPELLS, WISHES & DREAMS

SPELLS AND WISHES™
BOOK SIX

MARTHA CARR

MICHAEL ANDERLE

DISRUPTIVE IMAGINATION

LMBPN Publishing
2375 E. Tropicana Avenue, Suite 8-305
Las Vegas, Nevada 89119 USA

Version 1.00, June 2024
ebook ISBN: 979-8-88878-236-1
Print ISBN: 978-1-64971-998-0

THE SPELLS, WISHES & DREAMS TEAM

Thanks to our JIT Readers
Christopher Gilliard
Diane L. Smith
Jan Hunnicutt
Dorothy Lloyd

Editor

SkyFyre Editing Team

CHAPTER ONE

The entire room trembled violently, each tremor breaking chunks of stone away from the domed ceiling. Charlotte cried out and instinctively covered her head with her hands as they crashed to the floor in the center of the chamber. Smaller shards rained down on her as they splintered off the fallen debris and arched through the air.

Pain and rage filled the wyrmling as it shook its colossal head, as if it could cure the jolt caused by the impact with the wall. With a frustrated growl and eyes that had yet to adjust to the darkness, the beast shot straight up toward the dome as it searched for open sky, but it only met with more stone. Before it could assess its surroundings, it crashed headfirst into the ceiling with a deafening *crack*.

Rolling out of the way, Charlotte narrowly missed another barrage of stone falling around her. Looking up, she saw a spiderweb pattern in the stone, reaching broadly all around the beast's head where it had impacted the ceiling.

For a moment, the fairy godmother could only stare up at the enormous creature, propping herself up with both hands. At first, she thought she might be in luck, that it had knocked itself unconscious. After all, even with its massive size, she couldn't imagine how anything could suffer such a blow and not render itself instantly inert.

Charlotte's eyes widened as she realized the wyrmling was now falling away from the domed ceiling. She'd lost herself in the chaos, unable to look away, but now she needed to move, or risk being crushed beneath the wyrmling.

Adrenaline raced through her, forcing her into action. "Cat!" the fairy godmother called out as she leaped to her feet and dashed toward the perimeter of the chamber.

A gust of wind shoved against her back as the creature's swiftly growing shadow darkened everything around her. Remembering her wings had returned, she used them to quicken her pace as she surged toward the opposite wall. The thick stone approached much faster now, and to keep from rushing face-first into it, she used her wings to stop her short between a set of arched doorways filled with shimmering, opalescent sludge.

The world-shattering crash she expected to come as the wyrmling dropped like a stone to the chamber floor never came. She spun to find that the creature hadn't lost consciousness at all after bashing its head against the ceiling but had dazed itself long enough to interrupt its ability to fly. After falling most of the way back down, it now twisted and thrashed in the air to shake off the daze.

"Cat, where are you?" she called out, hoping to find her

companion before the beast regained its senses and things got worse.

A furious bark came from somewhere to her right, and she caught a glimpse of Cat's shaggy black form sprinting across the chamber toward her.

Charlotte's eyes bounced back and forth from Cat to the wyrmling and back again. As her eyes once again landed on the beast, she saw it had righted itself, and its focus locked on her. She stared with wide eyes at the wyrmling's opening maw as it coiled in the air and stalked toward her.

This place is too small for the magic I need to fight this thing as I usually would. I don't think it's hungry. I think it's pissed.

Suddenly, an idea came to mind, though she'd have to pull it off without a hitch. A single misstep would mean failure, and she wouldn't have a second chance.

As the wyrmling prowled across the chamber, she noticed that every couple of seconds, it winced and dropped several feet before climbing higher again. If she were a betting woman, she would bet it had a splitting headache after ramming headfirst into a stone wall and then again into the stone ceiling. She wondered if the pattern was caused by the cadence of the throbbing in its skull.

The fairy godmother used the beast's condition and slow, predatory approach to scan the perimeter. She searched for the doorway with the image of the field and *The Castle on the Hill*, where the wyrmling had come from. Her eyes darted around the room to locate the correct arch as she tried not to panic. The creature cried out and twisted painfully in the air, once again distracted by the pain.

The momentary lapse gave her the few seconds she needed, and she spotted it. It was almost directly across the room from her and slightly to the left of the wyrmling. Just as she started to work out a plan to get over there to lure the creature back in, it coiled like a snake, preparing to battle its way out of what it probably thought was a trap.

This particular wyrmling was a juvenile, but Charlotte doubted if even fully grown wyrmlings possessed the capacity for rational thought.

I'll have to help it along.

The wyrmling circled one last time from the opposite side of the chamber, its turquoise scales glinting beneath the refracted light from dozens of opalescent doorways. Charlotte raised her wand, taking a moment to catch her breath while waiting for the wyrmling to make its move.

For this to work, she had to catch it off guard. If it figured out at the last second that she was a more significant threat than she seemed or if it changed course, the fairy godmother would miss the only opening she'd get.

Time seemed to slow as the wyrmling uncoiled, its black eyes flashing red as it leveled its gaze on her once again. Charlotte lifted her chin and planted her feet squarely on the floor, silently daring it to come at her.

Don't worry, Beastie. You'll be home soon, and we'll be safe.

Cat's low growl rose from Charlotte's right, but she remained perfectly still, paying him no attention for fear the wyrmling would choose that very moment to strike. As with most predators, staring directly at it seemed to translate as a challenge, and she didn't want her opponent to think she had any plans to back down or leave herself open.

"Wait for it," she whispered to herself and Cat to remind them both to have patience. Taking another breath, she challenged the beast directly. "You want me? Come get me!"

Taking Charlotte's lead, Cat let loose a loud growl that echoed off the walls and sounded far more menacing than usual. As expected, the wyrmling accepted the challenge and responded exactly as Charlotte wanted.

It charged.

A blast of hot air surged their way as the wyrmling changed directions and growled, its hot breath blowing in her direction. The guttural sound boomed, causing a tremor through the floor, and she imagined it radiated through the walls and ceiling as well.

It started toward her, slinking through the air as if hunting her before picking up speed. Even from the great distance between them, the gusts of air coming from the whipping tail were definitely enough to knock her over if she allowed it to get much closer.

Her dress and cloak billowed around her as her hair blew back over her shoulders. Her gossamer wings pulled back to shield them from the heat and from catching wind when the beast drew closer, but she knew she had to act fast.

Charlotte briefly looked down at Cat to make sure he was still present and safe. His fluffy fur stood on end, and his head lowered as low warning growls continued to rumble from his throat. As her head turned back, a large lock of hair blew in her face, obstructing her view momentarily, and she quickly tossed it back before raising her wand.

The wyrmling bobbed in the air, occasionally changing its flight pattern from up and down to side to side, likely assuming this would disorient its foe. It toyed with her, now pausing in the air to circle back.

What the hell is it doing?

Charlotte was no ordinary opponent, but if it was trying to confuse her, its plan was working. One thing was certain. No matter what this thing chose to do, she would let no harm come to Cat, which meant protecting herself with just as much determination. She refused to become prey.

The wyrmling circled again and charged toward her. This time, its face contorted with intent. In no time at all it made it a third of the distance across the chamber, and Charlotte drew a deep breath, summoning all her strength, focus, and inherent magic.

As the beast reached the halfway point, a deep, ruddy glow bloomed at the tip of the fairy godmother's wand, casting her and her companion in red. The color glowed brightly in the wyrmling's eyes, and she had to force herself to look away, to focus on the beast as a whole.

At the two-thirds mark, the wyrmling opened its jaws to let out another deafening screech that ricocheted off the walls, piercing Charlotte's ears and making her eyes water. Cat snarled at the creature, solidifying his footing as if he planned to take it down all by himself.

The wyrmling's massive jaws remained open as it breached the three-quarter mark toward the fairy godmother. She waited until the perfect moment to strike, at the last second when the beast wouldn't be able to turn away.

The deep red glow at the tip of Charlotte's wand flashed with blinding intensity before expanding into a wall of light in front of her. The wyrmling crashed head-first into it, shoving Charlotte back several feet and screeching in pain as its body folded in on itself from how fast it had been moving.

She hissed in sympathy for the creature. Despite the fact that it was trying to kill them, she knew it was only because it was confused and scared, and that was a recipe for disaster with any creature, magical or otherwise.

The wyrmling only briefly hit the ground before twisting and lifting into the air once again. It flipped and twisted violently in the air, and she wondered if it was trying to shake off the pain. She didn't have to wonder for long.

The moment it righted itself, its head whipped around before its body followed suit, its eyes focused solely on her.

The wyrmling surged forward again, furious and terri-fied. Charlotte knew her barrier couldn't take another hit like it just did without channeling more magic into it, and she was never sure just how much magic she had. It seemed to have a mind of its own.

Lifting her wand, ancient words from a spell Charlotte had not used in ages welled up within her. As she began the incantation, the words flowed from her mouth in the old EverAfteran tongue, a language that was older than the Fairy Godmothers' Guild.

While she could no longer translate the spell from the old language to English, she knew the spell by heart and what it did. That was all that mattered to her right then as the words boomed from her mouth.

Gusts of air from both the wyrmling's approach and Charlotte's manipulation of immense magical power filled the chamber. This was unlike any power she had used in a very long time. Her cloak whipped around her as the wall of red light brightened and solidified just before the spell reached completion with the final word crashing through her lips.

"Cat, stay with me!" she shouted when she saw him lunge and snap with a loud, threatening bark. She knew he was likely trying to distract the creature, but it was too dangerous.

The wyrmling screeched again, causing Charlotte to wince against the pain ringing in her ears as the intensity of her spell reached a roaring crescendo. Soon, it drowned out every other noise, including the wyrmling's screech of rage.

Charlotte's arm burned as she tried to finish the powerful spell. Words weren't the only necessity. The spell itself was active, but to fortify and lock it, she needed to make specific movements with her wand. The wyrmling was almost upon her, its nauseating breath and the cloying heat it produced overwhelming her senses.

When she completed the final flick of her wand, the wall of red glowing light in front of her let out a deafening boom that echoed around the chamber. The light surged forward like an impenetrable wall to meet the wyrmling head-on.

The impact was almost as rough and disorienting as the beast's previous mistake of bashing its head against the chamber's domed ceiling and definitely as hard a hit as its first strike against the barrier. The fairy godmother's magic was more potent than the wyrmling, and the wall of light crashed into its snout with a horrifying thud.

The creature screamed as its face scraped along the much stronger wall of magic, which shoved it backward across the cavern and boxed it in on all sides. The wyrmling spun in a tight coil, preparing to strike again, only to be thwarted repeatedly by the fairy godmother's spell.

With each terrified screech, the wyrmling thrashed against the barrier, unable to gain momentum to attack or escape as its available space shrank by the second.

Charlotte was unable to aim the beast directly at the single open archway in the chamber from which it had emerged. Directing a spell that large was a bit harder than it was to aim a smaller one. She could send it in a general direction, but it was harder to steer.

Before the wyrmling could move within the shrinking magical box, Charlotte had to redirect her spell. With one step forward, both arms raised, and using strength from her whole body, she moved the spell slightly to the left toward the open archway leading into the valley beneath *The Castle on the Hill*.

Both her arms burned from the effort. Magic was more than just a wand. It required a connection, mind *and* body, between the godmother and her magical tool. It felt as though she were lifting the weight of the box and the wyrmling inside with her bare arms instead of with magic. She bellowed a battle cry against the forces had summoned, and it seemed to help her efforts.

She thought it felt like trying to throw a felled tree trunk over her head. Yet somehow, she made it work.

The enclosed magical box continued to glow red as it surged to the left, bashing the wyrmling against one of the other archways. Charlotte took another step forward and screamed once again as she pushed with all her might, giving her spell an extra nudge to reroute it.

The entire chamber shuddered again, and cracks in the walls widened as more chunks of stone dropped from the ceiling. Wind, heat, and powerful magical energy whipped back and forth across the room, making her job far harder because of how difficult it was to concentrate.

But when opposing forces fought against Charlotte Weaver, she pushed back more fiercely than ever before.

Slowly, one foot in front of the other, she made her way through the chamber, directing her magic to where she needed it to go. She felt as though she was marching through hardening mud toward the center of the chamber, while shoving the shrinking box forward. Inside, the screeching wyrmling thrashed about.

Finally, Charlotte lined the red, glowing magical box up with the correct archway. She took two more steps forward and pushed as hard as she could, shoving the wyrmling back through the archway. The magical box the fairy godmother had conjured squeezed through the opening before exploding on the other side.

The pressure and resistance Charlotte had fought against since initiating the spell snuffed out in an instant, and she stumbled forward with nothing there to catch her. She landed on her hands and knees with a loud *oof* and collapsed from exhaustion onto her hip in a sitting position.

She looked over to find Cat only a few feet away and realized he must have been walking directly behind her, supporting her as she wielded all that magic.

Without warning, the shockwave from her spell's explosion ricocheted back through the archway, knocking Charlotte all the way over and hitting Cat broadside, sending him rolling several times. The shockwave continued into the chamber and smashed against the circular stone walls before moving up along the domed ceiling. Dirt and various-sized chunks of rock rained down in every direction.

Charlotte quickly righted herself into a sitting position as she acted on instinct, raising her wand above her head and launching a blindingly bright silver dome of magic around herself and Cat to shield them. Cat barked continuously at the chaos while rubble pummeled the dome, sending ripples of light racing from points of impact. Cat panted heavily with anxiety as he made his way over to sit next to the fairy godmother. They were safe and relatively unharmed.

Though both of them had suffered quite the scare.

As quickly as the explosion had erupted in the chamber, the violent magical backlash of her powerful spell dissipated. The howling wind snuffed out, and the vortexes of churning dirt and pebbles vanished, dropping the smaller debris to the floor with tiny clacks.

A final chunk of stone fell from the ceiling, crashed onto the shimmering silver barrier, then split in two before rolling down the dome and landing on the floor, wobbling as they came to a standstill.

All was calm again except for Charlotte's racing heart, rapid breathing, and Cat's low, continuous whine. The threat seemed to be over, but that left Cat feeling the effects of everything that had happened. His body trembled against her, and she reached out to hold his giant head closer to hers.

As she did, she realized just how weak the arm that held her wand was. Compared to the free hand that held Cat, it was practically unusable. It was like she'd slept on it, and now it was useless until the feeling returned. Her entire limb trembled from shoulder to fingertip as she lifted it slightly, only for it to drop limply at her side.

The weakness and inability to keep her arm extended snuffed out the magic fueling her shield, and the bright silvery dome splintered into thousands of glittering pieces as it fell away from Charlotte and Cat.

For a moment, the pair sat in the center of the chamber, Charlotte catching her breath while Cat sniffed the air for signs of additional threats. And she was grateful nothing else presented itself right then because she wasn't entirely sure she could even lift her arm, let alone battle anything else.

The fairy godmother heaved an enormous sigh of exhaustion and relief before collapsing back on the chamber floor again. Her dark hair splayed out around her as she stared up at the dome above them, thinking about what had happened and how inspecting the archway nearly got them killed.

Finally, she looked over at her furry companion. When

she spoke, her words were breathless. "Art is lovely, and I think appreciating it is incredibly important. However, next time I see and then stare for too long at something moving around on the other side of a magical archway, or painting, or anything else, please remind me of this very situation."

Cat let out a quick, high-pitched whine, then flopped down next to the fairy godmother, looking at her with wide brown eyes. He shoved his snout into her free hand and offered a long, slobbery kiss of gratitude and reassurance.

"Well, thank you for that," Charlotte replied with a laugh that echoed quietly around the semi-destroyed chamber. "You're very sweet, and I appreciate you very much. Honestly, I have to say that we make a great team."

CHAPTER TWO

Though he had managed to hold himself together during half of their party's departure, Sir Thomas was incensed. Lady Charlotte and Cat had all but abandoned him, it seemed. Thanks to the detective and his inability to travel through enchanted walls like the rest of them in his current magically induced unconscious state.

The longer Sir Thomas sat around doing nothing, the more upset he became. He should be with the adventurers—adventuring! He should be solving puzzles with Lady Charlotte and Cat in the quest cave.

Not stuck there with the detective, who annoyed Sir Thomas on his best day but who had become a complete and total bore now that he lay prone, surrounded by a spell the fairy godmother had created before she ran off with Cat.

Sir Thomas felt like he may as well have been sitting there alone.

He had done his best to keep his thoughts to himself

because of something he remembered Alex telling him before.

Charlotte had discovered something called *streaming.* Sir Thomas had only recently learned about video cameras and such, and TV took that to a whole new level. Alex recommended a show about detectives that she might like, and she watched one after another.

In one of them, a suspect on the loose had seriously injured a young woman, and she barely survived. She was in a coma, and her family talked to her unconscious form while she lay there.

Sir Thomas found that to be rather ridiculous and unrealistic. In EverAfter, he thought magic might carry their words into their subconscious, but it was strange that humans did such a thing in a magicless world.

It was then that he learned that injured or sick humans in this world who were in such a state might still be able to hear their loved ones on some level. Charlotte found it fascinating, but Sir Thomas just found it strange. One more oddity about humans he didn't exactly care to know.

Little did he know he would end up in a situation where such knowledge would come in handy.

However, it *severely* limited his activities since there was a chance that Detective Taylor could still hear and feel things, that the human was still aware of his surroundings.

The longer Sir Thomas waited, trying to squash his frustrations into a tight little ball unbefitting of a sworn feline of the Swashbuckling Order, the more his fury grew. Lady Charlotte should have left Cat with the detective! Not Sir Thomas.

Finally, unable to simply sit and push a pebble around

on the cave floor with his paw anymore, he lost his capacity for patience and self-control and exploded into a verbal tirade that, under different circumstances, probably would have even made Cat turn and leave the room.

Cat wasn't here, nor was Lady Charlotte. All Sir Thomas had was this human detective floating three feet above the ground in front of him, nearly matching Sir Thomas' own height.

"I don't understand. After all I've done to help protect and aid the good lady, and she leaves me with the human? The boring, *unconscious* human at that." He turned to Alex. "Though, I suppose I do prefer you quiet than constantly giving me a hard time."

He grumbled as he began to pace the length of Alex's still form, clasping his paws behind his back. "All my experience, all my expertise... I'm a skilled swordsman and deadly with a knife. *Nothing* is happening here! She should have *wanted* the added protection when traveling through unknown parts of the cave.

"All the assignments and missions I've successfully completed for the Swashbuckling Order alone make me a *far* better questing companion than that cat-turned-giant mongrel. Though, Cat is quite delightful and a wonderful companion. It's just that I serve more purpose. It's hard to say when he will tuck tail and run or charge unprepared into battle. That could put Lady Charlotte in even *greater* danger! I have proven myself to Lady Charlotte time and time again, and I am relegated to the role of *human babysitter*."

He scoffed as he turned on a dime toward the detective, outstretching his paws as he gestured to Alex. "I'm not even here to keep him occupied!" His arms fell limply to his sides. "No. I'm supposed to simply sit here and watch his motionless body in hopes nothing happens to it. What's going to happen to it? Charlotte spelled it herself! He's completely shrouded in magic, and we saw how solid it is when he rammed into a wall instead of following the lady through."

He inhaled heavily through his nose in silence for a moment, crossing his arms and tapping his boot on the floor in annoyance. "This is ridiculous. If something *does* go wrong, I most certainly do *not* have the requisite knowledge or ability to patch holes in a fairy godmother's spell. I can't even call out to her to come back and make the repairs. If something like that were even possible."

He paced again, allowing his thoughts to process out loud. "I mean, would a hole or crack appear if it were damaged? Or would the whole thing collapse? Then again, maybe it could weaken over time before simply fading away. Ugh! See? I don't have a clue what I'm doing." He shook his head angrily. "Though, I suppose Cat wouldn't either. Still, I would have made a far better questing companion than his furry behind."

Sir Thomas paused his rant as he looked at the floor. He kicked a rock a few times as he slowed his pace, his attention oddly focused on the tiny thing as he batted it around with his boot and paced more slowly.

His ears perked when he heard what sounded like a bark, and he sharply inhaled. "Cat?" he called out semi-quietly. While he wanted to yell for his friend, he also didn't want to alert anything to their position in case anything really was lurking in the shadows somewhere. "Cat?"

He listened for several moments but heard nothing else. Just as he was about to give up hope it had been them on their way back, he thought he heard a feminine voice, but it was too quiet, too far away to make out what it said.

"Lady Charlotte?" His heart rate picked up. If she was calling for him, was it because she needed help finding them? Was she in danger? He didn't like that last thought at all. "Lady Charlotte, can you hear me?"

Nothing.

He sighed and rolled his eyes before turning to the detective. "You're not even awake, and you're driving me crazy. Look at me! I'm hearing things now."

The more he thought about it, the more it upset him. And his supposed "best friend" had run off in an instant with no consideration for how he felt at all.

"Cat, you furry bastard! You traitor—actually, no. That's taking it too far." Even in his anger he realized Cat was no traitor and calling him such was wrong. He prided himself on his honesty among friends, and he wouldn't lie about something like that, even to himself. "But still, he put me on the spot on purpose. Threw me under—" He paused, his furry tan brows creasing in thought. "What's that phrase humans use? Under the rug? Cat threw me under the rug? No. That doesn't sound right— Anyway, it's something like that."

"Either way, you—" Sir Thomas spun around quickly. He thrust a furry finger at the unconscious Detective Taylor only to see the transparent glowing magical box Charlotte had put him in inching away. "What the—?"

Sir Thomas rushed forward and pushed on the box, finding it surprisingly easy to move. He put it back in its original place and watched it for several moments to make sure the detective wouldn't go anywhere.

"This is exactly what I'm talking about. You, sir, are potentially the most highly guarded human in the history of your kind. You should be flattered, honored even, to be the sole focus of my time and energy in this place. This is a quest cave. It's meant for *questing*. Not *sleeping*, Detective. But no. Thanks to *you*, all either of us has accomplished so far is to walk through a tunnel filled with blue ore. All you had to do was push forward and not ruin it. Not do anything humanish. Well, at the very least humanish from *your* world."

He scoffed again. "What a place. No magic. It creates more problems than anything, it seems. Not to mention, it makes all your kind incredibly weak. If you couldn't even handle a tunnel, what exactly did you plan to do when things *actually* got hard in here? Huh? You've forced us to leave Lady Charlotte largely unprotected, you know. You're laying here taking a damn nap, and she's navigating through here alone—and no, I do *not* count Cat because she can't even communicate with him. Neither of you can."

He fumed again; his brief distraction gone now as his heart raced again with ever-growing anger. *Get the man next to some glowing blue anything, and he falls apart completely. I'd like to see how he'd handle going up against a monster of some kind!*

"And because of your predicament, I must remain here, ever vigilant, cursing that furry canine friend of mine because he assumed I would be the best candidate for the job. Ha! Me, the babysitter."

Sir Thomas tsked and shot another disapproving look at Detective Taylor, enshrouded in the fairy godmother's bright, silvery protective magic. For a good hour after Charlotte and Cat had left, Sir Thomas paced the cavern, keeping the detective's floating body away from the blue light of the ore.

His fury and outbursts of indignant ranting filled the time since he couldn't do much else. Eventually, with no one around to hear or scold him, Sir Thomas' energy settled. His anger ran out of steam.

Once it did, it was easier for him to acknowledge what Cat and Charlotte had set out to do. The talking cat still had no idea why Detective Taylor had started to float away, but if it had been Cat there, he wouldn't have been able to redirect him back. The spell made Alex light as a feather, but if the spell could only take so much damage, Cat likely would have used it all up while banging him off walls on the way back.

Not to mention Cat's uncanny ability to sense danger...

No, it had to be Sir Thomas who stayed with the detective. Charlotte would need that extra warning of danger more than Sir Thomas would while sitting in a quiet tunnel. And thinking like that allowed him to somewhat appreciate his task. Detective Taylor was, after all, part of their team.

Before the man had opened his home to Charlotte, Sir Thomas, and Cat, it had been a little worse for wear but comfortable, with a couch big enough for Sir Thomas to curl up on. There had been no shortage of full meals and occasional snacks, courtesy of Detective Taylor. The conversations sometimes baffled Sir Thomas, especially between Detective Taylor and Charlotte, but they rarely involved him or Cat.

More importantly, Detective Taylor had opened his mind and heart as well as his home, accepting two misplaced EverAfterans and one enchanted dog without requiring explanations or demanding they change.

Sir Thomas was certain that Detective Taylor might always be the sole human on whom any EverAfteran in distress could truly depend. The man had fulfilled his duties as an officer of the law in his world and attempted to uphold laws and regulations for EverAfterans in Cincinnati as well. And while they drove each other crazy, Sir Thomas knew they'd each fight to the death to protect the other.

Thinking about that made him feel a little guilty regarding his earlier rant.

Sir Thomas spun around at the end of the path he'd paced multiple times and headed back toward where Alex floated, gesturing toward the prone detective wrapped in glowing silver with a wave of his furry paw. "Seeing as I *choose* now to operate under the assumption that you can, in fact, still hear me, Detective, I will tell you about a saying among my kind. The upright, talking felines in our world aren't all from the Swashbuckling Order. However, those who came before me were certainly adventurers in their own rights. The saying has stuck with me all my life since it was first passed on to me in such words of wisdom."

Sir Thomas thrust a finger into the air as he switched

directions in his pacing, his other paw resting behind his back. "'A cat is only as strong as his mind is sharp.'" He glanced at the detective, but the human's state remained unchanged. Undeterred, Sir Thomas continued. "Obviously, you aren't EverAfteran, you aren't a talking cat who walks on two legs, and you most certainly are no swashbuckler. However, you are a brave human with virtue and an honor system of your own, and I can appreciate that about you, so I believe this applies to you. Even if you do make my whiskers twitch multiple times a day."

He stopped beside Detective Taylor's head, close enough now to peer through the shimmering silver light to see Alex's calm, peaceful features upon a floating bed of magic.

"It's strange. Physically, I see nothing wrong with you. You look very much asleep." He thought for a moment. "Perhaps I was a bit too harsh earlier. After all, it isn't like you've been around magic much, especially the true kind. Lady Charlotte has pulled off minor spells many times in your presence, but compared to what she's *truly* capable of, you've seen nothing. Honestly, thinking back, we probably should have seen this coming."

Sir Thomas' thoughts wandered back to the other times Detective Taylor had been around raw, powerful magic, and there were signs.

The transference warp. The barrier between Ginger Haus' human home and her cottage sitting on a magical nexus. The stone. All of them showed he had a sensitivity to magic. All of them showed a pattern we ignored.

"Hmm. You had physical reactions to several things before. Unfortunately, I don't know if it's because humans from your world simply *can't* handle magic or if magic is something all humans need to ease into. Something they adapt to over time. That would be a question for Lady Charlotte, no doubt, though I don't know that she would have an answer either. Considering she's never mentioned it, I would venture to say she wouldn't."

The magical cat stared into Detective Taylor's resting face, his furry eyelids narrowing as he studied the sleeping man.

"Even knowing you were uncomfortable physically and mentally, you made your oath and continued in here without knowing what might happen to you. That's either incredibly brave or incredibly stupid, Detective. Maybe a bit of both."

After a few more moments of thought, Sir Thomas left the detective for another round of pacing in the tunnel. "It's incredibly difficult to have one-sided conversations, though I must say, you not arguing with me every thirty seconds and me being able to actually speak is quite nice."

He cleared his throat, clasped his paws behind his back, and proudly straightened as he marched back and forth along the length of Alex's body.

"Anyway, as I was saying before... That saying was passed on to me through my ancestors and is something we live and die by. Any being worth their salt in whatever skills or values they hold dear cannot be of service to anyone else if they do not first care for themselves. As you train your body, you train your mind. One cannot surpass the other, or you'll find yourself limited in the direst of situations at some point.

"What good is all the mental swiftness in the world if

you aren't physically capable of pulling off whatever grand plan you hatched? And what good is all that strength and skill if you don't have a clue how to put it all to use? Sure, you could take on a large group and hope for the best, but a strong mind will have you through that situation in no time with as little trouble as possible."

He sighed and shook his head, feeling like he was getting off-topic once again. "I raged against Lady Charlotte's decision to leave me here with you as your personal protector. However, had I fought tooth and claw to refuse the role set upon me by a fairy godmother to whom I swore my oath, I believe it would have gone against everything I was taught because I failed to see the wisdom in it. After all, how would Cat have told you where Lady Charlotte and I were if you woke up? How would you have known everything was okay?"

His furry brows knitted together as he paused his steps to look upon Detective Taylor's face again. "You wouldn't have, which is why I was wrong. I will not abandon you in your time of need. Besides, I am quite certain that Lady Charlotte would skin me alive if she discovered I merely shirked all sense of loyalty and decorum and abandoned you here. Even if it was to move on to other far more engaging and entertaining adventures while trying to help the good lady and Cat.

"You are one lucky human, Detective. Your present circumstances notwithstanding, you have the best of the best at your side. That will not change until Lady Charlotte and Cat return to us and relieve me of my duty. Hopefully, by that point we will have discovered our next steps in this shared quest of ours and a way to extract you from within the depths of whatever enchanted sleep has taken you under."

With nothing more to share, Sir Thomas stopped pacing, which led him back to Detective Taylor's side. He looked at the human shrouded in silver light one more time and nodded as if Detective Taylor had thanked him for his protection during their surprisingly anticlimactic journey within the magical quest cave.

"Think nothing of it, Detective. That being said, if you were pleased with the job I did, I wouldn't turn away a celebratory outing. Perhaps even something along the lines of a lobster dinner? Of course, it would need to be freely given. While I would accept such an offer as an appreciative, friendly gesture, asking for or receiving monetary or other payment would be wrong and something I would never do. Though none of that can happen unless you are awake, so I hope we can figure this out soon. As annoying as you can be, for some reason, I miss our squabbles. However, if you actually *did* hear that and decide to tell anyone, I'll deny it until my dying breath." He straightened his belt, which didn't need straightening. "Just...so you know."

He took a few tentative steps closer to the detective and frowned. "Well, I suppose it was worth a try."

CHAPTER THREE

After their close call with the wyrmling, which had clearly come straight out of EverAfter, Charlotte and Cat took a moment to regain their faculties and catch their breath. The fairy godmother rested on the cold stone floor of the circular chamber, hoping her body and mind would recover so the jitters from the battle would settle.

While she expected test after test—some mental and others physical—when choosing to enter the quest cave, she was also under the impression that their group would be whole, and she wouldn't have to go at anything alone. Even with Cat, the situation left her to battle that beast alone, and it took a toll.

She couldn't remember the last time she slept because she had no way of knowing what time it was. Even if she did, was it that time *here*? Was it that time in Ohio? She had no way of knowing how long they'd been in the cave because time worked differently in different worlds. They might have been here for days, but when returning to the human world, they'd realize they were only gone for thirty seconds.

All that mattered to her right then was Alex was safe, or so she chose to believe. Otherwise, continuing her journey might be even more difficult. It's difficult to concentrate on puzzles and riddles when your mind scatters in other places, and it seemed this place was *very* good at scattering thoughts.

And groups, she thought sarcastically with a hint of anger.

Wiping that from her mind, she closed her eyes for a moment. "I need to rest for a moment, Cat. My arm is next to useless, and I need to fix it, but I can't do it while I'm as I am right now. Once I recover a little, I can restore my arm and potentially use a spell to reenergize myself. Sleep would be more effective, but anything to help us get through these quests will do."

Cat settled beside her with a huff. A small dust cloud plumed around him as he plopped onto the stone floor, and he snorted in response before laying his head across her hip. He stretched his back legs behind as he nestled in and closed his eyes a moment, too.

Despite his relaxed posture, the Newfoundland's ears often twitched as he remained alert, listening intently to ensure nothing would catch them unawares again. Every slight sound that followed their battle made him lift his head, sniff the air, and let out a low warning chuff in case there was anything else in the chamber thinking of approaching.

Cat put off enough heat to compensate for the cold, unforgiving floor, and at some point, while half awake and half asleep, Charlotte had pulled her cloak up enough to ball it up and use it as a pillow. She found far more comfort than expected and dozed quite soundly, given her situation. She knew Cat's ears would pick up any disturbance far sooner than she would, and it allowed her to recover without intense worry.

And while it wasn't a sure thing, the spell she encased Alex in was *supposed* to alert her if it shattered or faded. While she didn't know if she was too far away or if the enchanted cave would interfere with the spell alerting her, she chose to have confidence in her magic as well as in Sir Thomas. This also aided her in resting more peacefully.

There was no way for her to know how much time she and Cat had to complete this part of their quest or if there was even a time limit. She also didn't know how long they'd traveled down the first corridor before finding the opalescent goo on the walls or how long she stared at the images in the archways before the wyrmling appeared.

Thinking about the potential time limit brought her back to consciousness, her eyes fluttering open as the ache of her body alerted her to just how stiff she was. She grunted as she moved, that grunt turning into a groan as she shifted.

Cat whined as he lifted his head and studied her.

"I'm okay. Just need to move around and fix what ails me." She forced herself to a seated position, using her good arm, and Cat followed suit. He seemed just as slow and stiff as she did, and his wide yawn didn't help him hide it. "How do you think they're doing back there?" she asked, gazing across the chamber at the archway where the wyrmling had disappeared.

The image of the open field and *The Castle on the Hill*—which had previously filled the archway—was gone. Her brows furrowed as she noticed a residual shimmer lingering, but it paled compared to the iridescent glow of the other archways filled with the shifting goo she still couldn't identify. Even if the wyrmling's archway had refilled with the same substance, it would be distinguishable by the chunk of stone missing from the upper right side, leaving a gaping hole.

Charlotte looked at the missing chunk and then looked around to take in the full chamber. "I don't know what to do from here. We defeated the creature, but where are we supposed to go now? We can't just turn around and go back through the tunnel." She sighed. "The wyrmling didn't leave anything behind. No gifts, boons, or clues. We're no wiser to our situation than when we first came in here."

Charlotte groaned even more as she forced herself to her feet. She stretched, wincing when her injured arm sent a twinge of pain through the elbow, up through the muscle, and into the shoulder. She massaged it with her good hand as she turned in the opposite direction, scanning the circular walls and the dozens of archways filling the enormous chamber with light.

"Uh… Wait a second." A bolt of muted panic shot through her as her head went on a swivel. Her heart rate kicked up as she realized something vital was missing. "No-no-no. Where's the tunnel?"

Cat whined again as he climbed to his feet and joined her in the search. Each of them spun around as they looked in all directions for the tunnel that was no longer there.

"Oh, this is bad. I didn't *want* to go back through the

tunnel, but had we wasted more time, it would have been nice to know we could check on the others. This is terrible. Now we *really* have to figure all this out."

Trying to calm her panic, Charlotte began a more intense inspection of the archways lining the walls. Each one glowed with that unknown substance, and while she could distinctly pick out the doorway with the chunk of stone broken off, she could not find the tunnel that had brought her and Cat here.

"Shit," she murmured, spinning first to the right and then to the left, her eyes widening as she realized with absolute certainty that she was *not* imagining things. "It can't be gone. We've been here the whole time. We didn't go anywhere else, and the doors… All the doors are…"

Cat yipped, and she quickly looked over at where he was standing. The area looked familiar, but it had changed entirely. Her jaw fell open as her feet slowly led her in his direction. Her eyes carefully scanned the wall, seeing the faintest outline of where the tunnel entrance had been, but now it was solid stone.

In case it was a magical trick, she reached out and pushed on the solid stone within the arched entrance, but she quickly found it was normal, natural stone. There was nothing magical about it outside of whatever trickery had placed it there. There would be no slipping through here. They were officially closed in with no way out.

Charlotte couldn't bring herself to say it out loud but seeing it with her own eyes was no less real than if she had voiced it. The mouth of the tunnel that had brought her and her companion to this chamber was gone. That was the simple answer.

"Damn!" she shouted as she slapped the wall. It hurt, but not as severely as if she'd punched it like she suddenly wanted to.

She turned and sighed as the large black dog sat at her feet. She studied the other archways as their only chance of success. Every one of them lined the circular walls of the chamber, spaced around ten feet apart. None offered images or movement, which she found annoying. How was she to know what to do next with absolutely nothing pointing her in any direction?

Charlotte tightened her grip on her wand, sending pain radiating up her arm again. She was ready to investigate every archway, if necessary, to find their way out. "Well, this seems unexpected, but I think we all knew something like this was possible given the fact it's a *quest* cave. Still, I can't say that I'm enjoying this as much as I expected. I think some things are better in theory than in practice." She turned to Cat and quirked one of her brows. "So that I know we're both seeing the same thing here... The tunnel no longer exists here, does it?"

Cat replied with a high-pitched yip, scrambling to his feet without taking his eyes off the fairy godmother.

"I suppose that's good enough." She offered him a gentle smile, feeling it was insufficient. But what else could she do? The fairy godmother and the enchanted dog were out of options until another one presented itself. All they could do was wait for something to happen.

Charlotte wrinkled her nose at the idea and placed her good hand on her hip. Sitting and waiting was never her strong suit. She made her own opportunities. If the tunnel had disappeared, surely something else would appear in its place. If not by its own volition, then by force. She refused to spend more time here than necessary. They'd spent enough resting.

"Well, that settles it then."

Cat stared up at her with brown eyes, his tongue lolling from his mouth as he panted. He didn't bark this time, but his expression made Charlotte suspect she could guess his thoughts.

"Yes, I know. Sorry. I'm used to thinking things through on my own. Don't get me wrong. You are a wonderful companion, but you and I can't communicate like you and Sir Thomas can or like I can with the other two." She paused. "That doesn't mean you can't understand *me*, though. Should I think aloud so you and I can stay on the same page? I might not be able to understand you word for word, but maybe I can learn to communicate with you better."

Cat stepped toward her and nudged his snout into the back of her hand.

She smiled. "I'll take that as a yes. All right. So, let's lay this out. The entrance to the tunnel we came through to get here no longer exists. Now we're stuck in this chamber." Charlotte turned in a slow circle, scanning each shimmering archway. "The gateway that brought us the wyrmling was obviously a direct portal into EverAfter and close to *The Castle on the Hill*. That's all real, which means each one of these archways potentially leads to somewhere completely different."

Her eyes narrowed as she continued to think aloud. "Maybe they're all different types of portals. They're nothing like what has been sucking EverAfterans from their homes and dropping them in Cincinnati. That portal is one of a kind. I *do* know that much. However, it's possible one of these leads to exactly where we need to be next. We just have to figure out which one it is and help it along in getting us there."

Cat puffed out a sigh through his nose as he suddenly became very interested in her side. He sniffed it rapidly like he was on the hunt for something.

The fairy godmother sucked in a sharp breath from both pain and surprise and lurched away from Cat's inquisitive snout, which had traveled high enough up her ribcage to nudge the tenderest spot on her right side.

She had forgotten about the wound there because she only felt a dull ache this whole time since her focus had first been on fighting off the wyrmling, then she'd succumbed to exhaustion, and now her focus was on finding a solution to their current predicament. The wound was much like a paper cut she once had. Invisible and blissfully—or mostly in this case—pain-free until she noticed the blood seeping from the tip of her finger.

Now, the searing burn in her ribcage returned, and Charlotte almost hesitated to look down at her own body to investigate what Cat had discovered.

"Thanks for that little reminder, Cat," she said through clenched teeth. "I appreciate you looking out for me, but maybe next time you could nudge a little more softly."

She groaned as she pulled her cloak back and looked at her side. A quick glance revealed the wound was more serious than she had thought. A large rust-colored stain had bloomed across her violet silk dress at the right side of her ribcage.

"Well, that's probably not good." She gingerly pressed her fingers against the stain to confirm it was still wet and sticky. "Running around with a gash in my side and bleeding all over the place isn't the best of ideas." She sighed, wincing in pain as she did. "I thought all I needed to do was fix my arm, but it seems I have more. I *really* hope I'm rested enough."

Staring at the bloodstain, Cat let out a low whine, licked his muzzle, and turned to face the dozens of glowing archways encircling them in the chamber.

"Please keep an eye out for any other potential threats, and I'll focus on patching myself up."

Grimacing at the constant burn in her torso, Charlotte examined the original tear in her dress, stained crimson. It wasn't as bad as she had expected, but she still hoped she wasn't too rusty on healing spells. She found a two-inch gash below her bottom rib, with blood and exposed flesh, but nothing more.

"Well, at least it's not covered in goo or filled with wyrmling venom or some other nauseating parting gift," she murmured. "Looks relatively clean, actually. All right, how exactly do I want to approach this?"

After clearing her throat, Charlotte readjusted her weak grip on her wand and pointed it at the wound. The intense pain in her arm didn't help and caused a slight tremor in her wand hand, but this wound needed to be fixed before the other since it required the most strength.

The angle was awkward, making the attempt even more painful as she twisted her torso to see the injury and aim accurately, but she managed it with a series of grunts. Charlotte gathered all the magic within and around her, channeled it into her wand, and cast the healing spell on her own flesh for the first time.

"Oh!" she exclaimed. With a small laugh, Charlotte widened her eyes. "It really isn't bad—just a little tickle. Honestly, I don't see what all the fuss is about over being healed by a fairy godmother. Everyone says it's painful, but this isn't bad at a—"

Her casual narration broke off in an ear-splitting scream as a flare of agonizing heat speared through her ribcage. A wave of dizziness overwhelmed her, followed by a worsening tremor in her wand hand as an instant sheen of sweat broke on her brow. Her eyes welled with stinging tears as her face scrunched in terrible pain.

A groan escaped her, then she lost the ability to speak as all her focus centered on keeping her wand pointed at the wound that needed healing despite the urge to stop.

Seconds later, her already weakened arm and hand shook even worse, though the tip of her wand stayed within the limits of the gash in her side. Charlotte blinked rapidly to clear the tears so she could watch the healing process until halfway through, when she could no longer bear to look. She clenched her eyes shut, gritted her teeth, and forced herself to continue. She had to do it.

It felt like an eternity, but she felt the exterior wound close once she'd healed the inside damage. The flare of magic and searing pain snuffed out at once, and her weakened arm fell limply to her side.

Charlotte gasped in relief and exhaustion, her knees weakening. As she sank onto one knee, panting and staring across the chamber, the fairy godmother was grateful she went for that wound before her arm because that took a lot more out of her than she'd expected.

Her vision blurred again as more tears filled her eyes and spilled down her cheeks. The pain was gone, but the shock, combined with the effort of concentrating on both the spell and not pulling away from her own healing, had drained her energy.

With another gasp, Charlotte bowed her head and waited for the sensations to subside. Her pulse slowed with deep, calming breaths, and she managed to open her eyes again, this time without tears. She used the back of her good arm to wipe them away from her face, and she cleared her throat.

"Good gods!" she exclaimed with a heavy sigh. "That is *nothing* like how our instructors described it in training."

With another low whine of concern, Cat padded over to her, looking the fairy godmother over from head to toe.

"I'm quite all right, Cat," she said, forcing out a bitter laugh. "Well, for the most part. I take back everything I ever thought about those brave adventurers who needed a fairy godmother's healing touch. It would seem none of them were overreacting."

When her companion still looked unconvinced, Charlotte smiled and extended her hand. Cat quickly accepted, poking his snout against her open palm and then licking her fingers with noticeable relief and delight.

"Thank you, Cat. I probably would have carried on for quite some time without addressing that issue, and I can only imagine how much worse the healing would have been had I waited any longer. Infection likely would have set in, and it would have been twice as hard to heal. You are one incredibly astute canine, my friend."

After several more happy kisses to her fingers, Cat finally pulled away, licking his chops before turning to face the dozens of shimmering stone archways again. He sniffed at the air and snorted.

"I need to fix my arm, and then it's time for us to investigate these archways. When all this is said and done, and both of our worlds are put back together the way they're meant to be, I should see if there are accolades and awards handed out to enchanted canines who involve themselves in a fairy godmother's magical missions. If there isn't already some medal or never-ending dog treat, I assure you, I aim to create one. You might even find yourself with an official title, like Sir Thomas. What do you think?"

Cat blinked at her, then snorted and turned away to pad across the chamber to investigate the other archways.

"Well, all right then. It doesn't have to be any of those specifically," Charlotte replied as she prepared to work on her arm.

Luckily, for this one, she only needed to reverse the magic from the wand into her wand hand and push it upward through her arm instead of casting it outward. She took several deep breaths, hoping this wouldn't be as involved as the wound in her side.

She whispered the words to herself and felt the moment the magic shot into her hand. It felt like having a hot fire poker trace up the limb, but it *still* wasn't as bad as her side, and she managed to keep any screaming to low groans.

Once the magic reached her shoulder, it bloomed

across the joint from front to back before it immediately stopped. The fairy godmother let loose a heavy breath before panting as she tried to calm herself. She blinked away a couple of more tears before pressing her lips into an *O* and then blowing out a final heavy breath.

"Okay. Well, I'm wide awake now," she mumbled before forcing herself to stand and dust off her dress. "The arm is as good as new, and I feel much better. As long as my energy holds out, I'm ready for whatever comes next."

She scanned the archways in front of them. "Whatever happens after this quest is over doesn't matter nearly as much as getting through it. Let's see if we can figure out what comes next so we can get ourselves out of here."

The two of them perused the dozens of archways cut into the stone of the circular chamber, but none contained any other blurry shapes or coalescing images like the wyrmling's archway. After closely inspecting half of them, Charlotte began to wonder if the archway through which the wyrmling had appeared was a fluke, or perhaps the only one leading out of this chamber.

If that's the case, then we've destroyed our only viable path out of here. She wasn't sure if the chunk that fell out when the wyrmling squeezed back through caused the first archway to darken, but there was certainly something different about it now. *If that's what happened, we may have doomed ourselves to spend the rest of our lives stuck in here.*

Charlotte shook her head, hoping to dispel her dark thoughts so she could focus on the facts. "Terrifying myself into thinking that was our only way out won't help us find a new way. Besides, what's that saying? When one door closes, another one opens? Something like that. It certainly fits our situation, doesn't it?"

Cat didn't pull away from his highly focused sniffing at the next archway to her right.

"Of course it does. And clearly, you aren't worried about our options being exhausted. So, if you're not worried about it, I won't be either. There is always a way, especially when a fairy godmother is on the scene. I can't forget that."

Cat didn't respond, which, oddly enough, filled Charlotte with a renewed sense of determination and urgency. The Newfoundland wasn't alarmed by their circumstances, and he didn't feel the need to dignify her thoughts with one of his usual responses. Somehow, that felt significant. Especially since his keen senses always seemed to find vital clues.

"Here we go, then," she said, brandishing her wand before shoving straight strands of hair back away from her face. "We'll find a way out of here one way or another."

Cat stopped sniffing the archway, where he'd focused his attention, snorted, shook his head, and trotted off to the next one to investigate further.

I think I'm starting to understand why Sir Thomas spends so much of his time talking with Cat. Somehow, it's quite a bit more practical than most conversations I've had in similar circumstances.

CHAPTER FOUR

The fur on the back of Sir Thomas' neck stood, and he looked around the tunnel. He walked the length of Alex's body and past it about ten feet, repeating the process at the detective's head. The cat's eyes narrowed when he found nothing.

He'd felt as though someone was watching him. Usually, his senses weren't off, but he also wasn't generally in an enchanted cave where anything could be messing with him and causing the reaction.

After gazing around the cavern one more time as if he still expected someone to be watching him, Sir Thomas returned his full attention to Detective Taylor. Particularly, the human's head and face hovering in the air in front of him, almost perfectly at eye level.

"I've never understood why you humans don't have fur outside of the small bit on your head. Honestly, how do you stay warm? Surely, clothing isn't as warm as a luxurious coat." He grumbled before continuing. "One of your own, not one a human steals from an animal."

Curiously, the cat reached out with both paws, hesitated for a brief moment, then settled them on the top of Detective Taylor's head. The brilliant silver light of Charlotte's magic protecting Alex flashed once with brighter intensity at Sir Thomas' touch. Then, both of his paws were allowed through the membrane of protective magic and settled down in Alex's hair.

"*Ooh...* This is much softer than I imagined. Hmm, I suppose if we were to call this mop on your head a coat, I would say yours is quite nice. I still think you should have a full coat, not the pathetic, thin little dark hairs on your arms like you have. Why even bother with those? And these eyebrow things... What is their purpose? Ugh!" He grew frustrated suddenly at the detective's lack of response.

Sir Thomas gripped Alex's head between both paws and vigorously shook it back and forth, though it barely amounted to more than his head bobbling side to side.

"*Wake...up...Detective!*" He emphasized every word with a slight pause between each. "You have to! Charlotte needs you."

Alex's body slightly wobbled as it hovered in the air, still surrounded by the shimmering silver protective magic. Despite Sir Thomas' efforts, the detective remained unresponsive.

He released the detective with a heavy sigh, scowling at the light enveloping him. "Well, it was worth a shot. There is little I can do for you right now, Detective, but I still wanted to try. I hope you don't miss out on the entirety of our shared quest because of being stuck like this." He paused, realizing he was getting a bit sappy with the detective again and cleared his throat. "If we can't manage to wake you, I imagine you'll force us to endure your constant whining about it for days to come. That doesn't exactly sound like a good time to me. The only sour moods I'm equipped to handle are Cat's, and those are short-lived and easily distracted."

Sir Thomas removed his paws and studied Alex a moment longer. He noticed the human's eyes shifting back and forth as if he was dreaming. *Interesting.* Sir Thomas found himself wondering what his companion might be dreaming about. He'd assumed, since it was a spell that had taken him under, that it would be a dreamless sleep. Much like the one Aurora had been under long ago.

However, it seemed as though he was mistaken.

The cat clicked his tongue and lowered himself to the cold stone floor of the cavern tunnel. The shuffling of his feet and every little sigh echoed within the area.

"You humans really are such fragile things. I wonder if Lady Charlotte knows any spell that might strengthen your constitution. Maybe give you some kind of efficient and long-lasting protection against magical ailments such as the one that, to be completely honest, took you down so quickly and easily."

Sir Thomas paused, expecting Detective Taylor's voice to respond to his remarks. Despite the obvious, some part of him still anticipated a quip from the human. However, as usual, since the spell had taken root, there was no response from Alex, and a surprisingly strong disappointment filled the talking cat because of it.

"I truly hope for a full recovery, Detective. This is most unlike you, and though I might have previously been grateful for silence during my explanations, I find myself rather sad and disappointed to see you like this. Perhaps even a bit fearful of the possibility that you may not—"

Sir Thomas' words choked off as he fought to hold back his suddenly overwhelming emotions. Without the other half of their party, their time in the tunnel had forced Sir Thomas to find ways to entertain himself. Talking was always a good thing for him, but he never expected his feelings to morph from anger and agitation to remorse, sadness, and a fierce determination to fulfill the role Lady Charlotte had bestowed upon him.

"Not to worry, Detective," he added quickly, swiping his paws across his eyes and blinking furiously. "You are in safe paws, and whether or not you can hear me now, I do hope you can detect the truth in my words. I mean every bit of it."

With a sigh, he looked away from the detective's floating body and stared at the cavern floor between his outstretched hind legs.

"What has gotten into me?" he whispered. "I'm thanking a human for his good deeds and offering promises that might put me in harm's way. I never would have believed it if someone told me this was on the list of things that would happen today." He sighed heavily. "Lady Charlotte, I hope you and Cat are having more success in your endeavors than we are here. I can only imagine how much more exciting your half of the mission is."

A faint *yip* sounded out, causing Sir Thomas' ears to flinch. His head jerked up at the sound, and he paused, waiting. *That sounded like Cat again.*

"*...Thomas... okay...*"

His brows furrowed when he heard Charlotte's voice but could barely make it out. He stood, struggling to pinpoint the direction it had come from. "Lady Charlotte?" he called out. "I can't hear you. If you can hear me, you have to repeat yourself."

He waited for several quiet moments, but there was nothing.

Deciding it was worth a risk just in case something was wrong, he inhaled deeply, filling his belly with all the air he could hold, and yelled as loudly as he could. "Lady Charlotte! Can you hear me?!"

He closed his eyes, really focusing to hear anything he could, but once again, only silence greeted him.

"Ugh!" he grunted with annoyance before kicking a rock as hard as he could down the tunnel. "Pointless."

Sir Thomas made his way back to the spot he'd vacated a moment before and flopped back down, wincing and leaning over to pull the small pebble he'd roughly sat on out from under his backside. A slow, gurgling grumble emanated from his stomach as he moved back to a comfortable position, letting him and any rodent or insect within hearing distance know of his hunger. He glanced down at his furry belly and frowned before looking back at the detective, his brows furrowed.

"Detective, it suddenly occurs to me that I *really* hope that sleeping spell or the protection magic around you keeps your necessary physical functions in stasis. Otherwise, guarding you will become far more unpleasant for both of us." His stomach growled again, and he rolled his eyes in annoyance. "Not to mention, there isn't a single edible...well, *anything* around here. Unless you keep a few snacks in the pockets of that ridiculous jacket."

He paused a moment, studying the detective before standing slowly and making his way over, almost as if he were prowling toward him, hunting him. "Well, since we're stuck here, and you wouldn't need them anyway... I might as well take a look. It can't hurt."

Though he'd stated his intentions, Sir Thomas still eyed Detective Taylor warily in case he or the magic around him deemed it an appropriate time for the sleeping curse to lift and Detective Taylor to come back to full awareness.

After another moment of silence from the human hovering three feet in the air, Sir Thomas nodded and made up his mind. "Okay...now to search the detective's pockets. Who knows? We might even discover some—"

Before Sir Thomas could finish his statement, the entire cavern shuddered violently, throwing him down onto his backside. A wild tremor passed beneath the floor, growling and rumbling as the smooth stone lining the tunnel quivered and rocked.

Sir Thomas steadied himself against the floor and decided to wait for the worst of the tremors to subside before attempting to stand again. Long, thick cracks ripped through the solid walls around him, causing his eyes to widen.

He peered up at the single bobbing orb of light Charlotte had conjured and left behind to avoid leaving them in complete darkness. From where he crouched, Sir Thomas could not see the cavern's ceiling, making it difficult to spot any potentially falling chunks of stone. Cracking sounds of rock prying away from the walls echoed around him, masking their true locations until they fell. Larger pieces of debris toppled around Sir Thomas and Alex, but fortunately, nothing hit them directly.

While Sir Thomas crouched low, waiting for the earthquake to abate, Detective Taylor remained unaffected by the tremors.

The cavern's rumbling groan against the violent rocking of the earthquake forced Sir Thomas to clamp his paws over his sensitive ears. When it finally did, he warily lowered his paws and looked around the empty, dimly lit space where the fairy godmother had instructed him to watch over Detective Taylor until she and Cat returned.

When no other tremors followed, he leaped to his feet and rushed to check Alex over.

"All right. Duly noted," Sir Thomas said to no one in particular, his voice echoing loudly in the cavern as he took in the detective's appearance to see Alex was unbothered by what had just happened. "I will not search his jacket pockets for snacks."

He scanned the semi-darkness again, then lowered a paw onto the grip of his rapier, frowning at the unconscious detective. "Another earthquake. I'm sure you didn't know this, Detective, but that type of earthquake is not supposed to reach all the way into a place like this. This is an enchanted quest cave in a magical place that resides between two worlds. We should be completely beyond anything that plagues either of our worlds.

"I can only assume this is something entirely different. Whatever it is, I won't leave you here alone. If all goes well and according to plan, Lady Charlotte and Cat should be finished with their part of things soon, and then we can complete our own, whatever that may be."

Feeling more reassured by his own comments meant for Detective Taylor, Sir Thomas gave a curt nod and spun around to scan the cavern. It seemed their first real threat had shown itself, though it was another one of the earthquakes the party had been aware of for several weeks.

Suddenly, Thomas felt more useful. Instead of merely acting as a placeholder while Cat and Lady Charlotte adventured through their quest cave, he now had the task of protecting the unconscious human detective from falling rocks.

A certain satisfaction filled Sir Thomas, and he paid far more attention to their surroundings. The sights, smells, and any sensation that alerted him that a magical disturbance may be in the air; he was likely to pick up on any of those at a moment's notice.

Instead of their previously familiar surroundings, a bright flash of warm orange light from his left greeted him. Sir Thomas turned to see the light quickly fading around the outline of a newly revealed stone archway leading into another corridor. It was similar to the archway through which Charlotte and Cat had left, though it lacked the strange cryptic writing neither of the EverAfterans recognized.

"Well, that's new." Sir Thomas took a few hesitant steps toward the archway, then glanced back over his shoulder at Detective Taylor, and then looked at the mouth of the tunnel filled with glowing blue ore from which their party had emerged hours ago.

"Taking you back through that tunnel is an obvious no-go, Detective, but this other archway didn't exist two minutes ago. I'm still unsure if leaving this spot is the right thing to do or not. For now, I imagine it's best if we stay here and wait it out. New doorways or not, more earthquakes or not, Lady Charlotte is expecting us to be right where she left us, and that's where we should stay until we know otherwise."

Sir Thomas tried to ignore the new stone archway that was giving off a soft, warm, orange glow. Folding his arms, he did his best to look anywhere but at the archway. However, its sudden appearance filled him with the distinct impression that it might be connected to the earthquake. The longer he waited for Charlotte and Cat to return, the more tempted he was to walk over, peer into the archway, and possibly even see it through. Even leaving Detective Taylor, if necessary.

No. Those are intrusive thoughts, and I'll never allow it to happen.

Sir Thomas crossed his arms over his chest and settled in, more determined to prove himself than before now that his own thoughts had threatened to betray everyone he held dear.

Even the human detective.

CHAPTER FIVE

"Hello?" Alex called out.

Everything suddenly went dark. It was like the light coming from the blue ore snuffed out at the same time as Charlotte's magical orbs. It was pitch black.

"Panicking already, Detective?" Sir Thomas poked.

Alex rolled his eyes even though he knew the cat couldn't see. "Not hardly. I just wanted to make sure everyone was okay. Charlotte?"

"Oh, I'm fine." Her voice held an edge to it.

"Are you sure? You don't seem fine." Detective Taylor wished he could go to her, but he knew moving would be the worst of ideas. He could end up falling into the wall of ore, and he had no idea what touching it would do to him. He wouldn't risk that or tripping into one of his companions and hurting them.

Charlotte grunted. "Yes. I'm... Yes! There it is!" She audibly sighed with heavy relief only a second before Alex saw a pinkish glow growing about ten feet away. "I couldn't find my wand."

She must have stuffed it in her Mary Poppins cloak, *he mused.*

Suddenly, three small orbs of light grew from the size of marbles to the size of softballs as they floated around her wand, and with the flick of a wrist, they shot into the air above them. Alex didn't think they would put off enough light in such pitch darkness, but the higher they flew, the brighter they became. They steadied around ten feet above them, slowly bobbing in the air as they cast light down in all directions.

"What happened?" Alex asked. "Seems kind of strange for everything to go dark like that, don't you think?"

Charlotte sighed before turning to him. "I don't know any more than you do at this point. Look, I know you're the only non-magical being here, but if I'm going to get us through here, I can't stand around answering a bunch of nonsense questions that won't help us along. Yes, it's strange. No, I don't know what caused it. Let's just keep moving and see what we can find."

Alex's eyes widened a bit. She'd never snapped at him like that before. She seemed fine a few minutes ago, just before everything went black. Now, she seemed irritated.

"Are you sure you're okay?" He lowered his volume, almost scared she would snap at him again.

The fairy godmother reached up and rubbed at her temples. "Yes, sorry. I'm just a little irritable. Quest caves are rare to come across and a great honor to complete. It's essentially EverAfter's way of testing you to make sure you're the hero you think you are, and it humbles those who only pretend. I do not want to be humbled here. Living in Cincinnati for months with no magic has humbled me quite enough."

Sir Thomas cleared his throat. "Detective, you need to remember how much responsibility sits on Lady Charlotte's shoulders. Not only is she the sole person here capable of using magic, but she is the sole person here who understands enchanted caves. *She has to navigate all this and solve puzzle after puzzle. If anything comes for us, it will likely be something that handgun of yours won't touch. That means she's the only one who can battle it. Well, aside from me, of course. I will always help defend Lady Charlotte. You, however–*" Sir Thomas shrugged. "*Sorry to say, but you are little more than useless, which leads me to my final point. She must do all those things while babysitting a defenseless human. One who is affected by absolutely anything with an energy signature.*"

Alex had had about all he could handle of that damn cat throwing his humanity in his face. Since when was it a bad thing to be human?

"Listen here, you little rodent—"

"Enough!" Charlotte barked. "Don't make me separate you two."

"*But can we anyway?*" Sir Thomas asked.

Exasperated, Charlotte groaned and stalked off, heading farther into the cave. The only thing that kept his mouth shut was the fairy godmother. It was apparent she was having a hard time, and he certainly didn't want to make it any worse for her.

Cat barked and darted ahead. One of the orbs broke away and followed him. The giant black furball didn't run far enough even to create a gap in the light, so Alex was able to see where he was at all times.

"Looks like there's a fork in the road," Alex noted.

"Seems that way," Charlotte breathed, though it seemed to be absentminded. Her head was on a swivel as she inspected each tunnel they'd discovered. One directly ahead, and one on either side. They were at a crossroads and would need to choose the next path they took. "Cat, do you have any suggestions? You seem to have a supernatural sense for all this. What do you think?"

The Newfoundland barked, the sound reverberating off the walls as he darted forward into the tunnel directly across from them. When he stepped across what served as its threshold, he spun once, tapping his front feet with excitement as his tongue lolled out to the side and his tail wagged with enthusiasm.

"Well, he seems awfully certain," Alex offered.

Sir Thomas nodded. "It's strange. Had he been a normal cat from EverAfter that Charlotte accidentally changed into a dog, it would make more sense. But he's an Earth cat. Earth cats have no knowledge of magic, and yet, Cat here seems to know things even Lady Charlotte does not."

Alex thought for a second, quickly realizing the talking cat was right. It was strange, but it worked, and that was all he cared about right then.

"All right, let's go. I trust Cat's judgment. We've already passed one obstacle. The blue ore was meant to stop us, but Alex made it through okay."

Sir Thomas snorted. "Barely. He got dizzy and almost passed out. A wall almost brought him down."

"Enough, Sir Thomas," Charlotte scolded, interrupting Alex before he could even get his mouth all the way open.

He was going to end up in a fight with that cat at some point. He just knew it. Today seemed like it might be the day because Thomas had more attitude than usual.

That was saying something.

Charlotte continued after giving the annoying talking cat the side eye. "Stop goading the detective. He can't help that he's a weak human any more than you can help that you're a bipedal cat. He serves a purpose in this group as well. I don't yet know what that is, but I'm sure it's something."

Alex's chest tightened. Sir Thomas gave him a hard time all

the time. That was normal. Even though it bothered him as a man to be ridiculed by a three-foot-tall talking cat, it didn't hurt emotionally.

What Charlotte just said gutted him.

She thinks I'm weak?

"Yes, you're quite wise, my lady. Carry on."

Alex's nostrils flared as he bit back the emotion welling. Something was wrong. Sir Thomas was always a jerk to him, but honestly, they were jerks to each other. Charlotte didn't have a mean bone in her body, so he couldn't figure out why she was so irritable and indifferent to him. Even going so far as to damn near call him useless.

Sure, she'd said he "served a purpose," but the fairy godmother also said she had no idea what that purpose was yet, meaning he was useless until proper usefulness popped up.

Without saying a word, Alex followed his group into the next tunnel. The orbs skipped along, the last one moving to the front of the line as they passed it to keep the path lit ahead. They seemed to have a mind of their own and a process they followed without any interference from Charlotte.

He found it fascinating, and he wondered if he'd get the chance to see her use her real power in here.

He didn't know how long they walked, but it seemed they'd reached the end of the tunnel, though he couldn't yet see what was up ahead. A low growl came from their guide dog, and Alex's eyes snapped forward. Cat's head lowered, his entire body creating a straight line from his nose all the way to the tip of his tail as he went on full alert.

"What is it, Cat?" Sir Thomas asked.

A rattling kss-kss-kss echoed through what Alex now realized was a large chamber when he stepped closer. The ceiling was *far taller than they'd been in the tunnels they'd traveled through. The light didn't reach the top, so it cast shadows all over.*

Another kss-kss-kss rattled even closer throughout the cavern, and for some reason, it chilled Alex to the bone. It creeped him out. Whatever it was had advanced on them, and it sounded big.

Alex was just about to suggest they turn around when the tunnel they still stood in rumbled. A stone wall slammed down behind them, trapping them where they stood. Charlotte spun, her eyes wide as she took in the wall behind the detective.

"No-no-no!" she cried out. "Not good."

"It appears the cave wants us to fight, my lady," Sir Thomas said, unsheathing his sword.

More rumbling came from the opposite side of the cavern as a doorway lifted, presenting a way through into another tunnel.

"There!" Alex pointed. "That's our way out."

"Typical human response," Charlotte breathed with annoyance.

"Excuse me?" Alex asked, confused again by the cruelty in her tone.

"Do you honestly *think it would be that simple?" She looked over her shoulder, her eyes meeting his as she quirked a brow incredulously. "Please tell me you aren't that dumb. This is a quest, Alex. Not a casual Sunday stroll. The* second *we step into this cavern—"*

A loud click *sounded, quickly followed by four to five more as eight legs connected with the floor, a couple of them at the same time as others. Alex thought his eyes might fall out of his head as his watched a spider that was no less than two stories tall.*

It was like a giant version of most other large species of Earth spiders, eighty percent legs. This one looked like a colossal yet slightly thinner black widow, but it was dark brown with an almost snakelike skin pattern. The body was the length of a city bus, and its rounded backside was as wide as two, maybe even three of them!

The fairy godmother sighed. "Yeah. That will happen. Fantastic."

Alex stared on in wide-eyed horror as the beast moved, each of its eight legs clicking against the floor. Charlotte seemed more annoyed than scared now, and he couldn't understand why she wasn't freaking out.

"And just what the hell are we supposed to do with that thing?" Alex asked.

"Invite it out to dinner," Sir Thomas quipped. "What do you think? Fight it. And you're a detective? I think the Cincinnati Police Department really needs to reconsider your employment. You're not very quick."

"It'll have to be me," Charlotte announced as she gripped her wand tighter. The spider stayed where it stood, seemingly waiting for her to approach. "I'm the only one with magic. Alex, just stay back. You'll be useless. I can't afford to babysit you while trying to focus on battle."

"I can at least try," Alex defended. God, she was being hard on him. It wasn't like her at all, and he couldn't understand. "Please don't fight me—"

"I said stay back!" she snapped. "I will not die in there because your fragile male ego won't allow a woman to save you. Back off."

His eyes widened, and she turned to step into the large chamber. The moment she did, that loud kss-kss-kss noise echoed off the walls again. It was always loudest when it started, fading off at the end, and it chilled the detective every time.

Please let their fight go okay, he thought as he pulled his gun from his holster and racked it. Out of respect for her wishes, he didn't yet click the safety off, but his thumb was right there, waiting just in case she needed him.

Without warning, Charlotte's wand glowed only a heartbeat before she cried out with the force of her swing. Several bright fireballs arced through the air, each one connecting with the spider's body and exploding on impact.

The creature gave a high-pitched wail that echoed off the chamber walls. Sir Thomas took the spider's distraction as his cue and ran for it. Alex started forward, and Cat spun on his heels, lowering his head and growling at him.

"What the hell, Cat?" The large dog gave a warning bark before jumping forward to push the detective back. "What are you doing? I'm just trying to get closer to see."

Cat growled again, and the detective felt even more flustered. He felt so lost. All his companions seemed irritated by his presence as if they didn't want him around. Like he was a burden. He started to wonder if maybe he was. After all, he was the only one who had no magic. All he had was his gun, and once the bullets were gone, he had nothing.

They're right... I'm in the way.

His heart sank as he looked up to watch Charlotte and Sir Thomas battle the eight-legged monster.

It stomped at her, its spiky leg spearing the stone floor and sending rock momentarily flying into the air before crackling down all around her.

Sir Thomas leaped and slashed his sword while the spider focused on what it assumed to be the larger threat: Charlotte.

The rapier hit one of the spider's long joints, and black blood sprayed everywhere just as the swashbuckling cat landed on his feet again.

"The other side now, Sir Thomas!" Charlotte called out just as she dove out of the way of another strike.

She tumbled over once and landed on her knees. Without hesitation, she swung her arm again, and this time, blue fireballs even hotter than the last arced up to land blow after blow into the spider's abdomen.

As instructed, Sir Thomas darted under the spider, dodging its strikes with its javelin-like feet with the agility gifted to him as a cat. As before, he leaped into the air and made another calculated slice through the air.

Another wail filled the cavern as more black blood sprayed out onto the floor.

"Cat! Alex!" Charlotte called out as she got to her feet to make her next attack. "Run for the door. Sir Thomas and I will keep it distracted!"

Cat immediately backed off Alex, yipped, and turned toward the chamber. He ran in and slowed to a trot as he skirted the edge of the room. Figuring the wonder dog would know the best route, Alex followed without complaint. He kept his gun at his side just in case he needed it.

Suddenly, the spider turned, its cold eyes locking on Alex and Cat.

"Go!" Charlotte cried out before launching another barrage of fireballs into the seemingly impenetrable abdomen.

Cat and Alex broke out into a full run, but Alex stopped cold when he heard a painful grunt followed quickly by a crack and cry of pain.

When he turned, he saw Charlotte lying on the floor by the

wall not far from their escape. She slowly rose to her knees, her eyes locking on his.

"Forgive me," she said.

His brows furrowed in confusion just as the spider wailed again. He glanced over to see Sir Thomas was successful in taking out a third leg, but that victory was short-lived as the spider used one of its others to swat the cat in a way Alex assumed it had done to Charlotte.

Sir Thomas launched across the room, but he didn't hit the wall. Instead, he hit the ground hard and rolled several times.

"Cat! To me!" Charlotte called.

Alex took one more look at the spider, who was once again focused on Charlotte before he darted toward her. Her eyes locked on his, and she shook her head.

Without warning, Alex's legs came to a startling halt as his feet rooted to the ground. He looked up at her with wide eyes.

"What are you doing?" he pleaded.

She shook her head. "I'm sorry. You're the only one without magic. There are three of us and only one of you." She rose, looking at Cat, who finally made it over to her, and Sir Thomas who was still gathering himself. "Get to the exit," she ordered.

The spider let loose a battle cry before charging at Charlotte. She looked at him with determination and confidence in her expression. "Goodbye, Alex."

Alex suddenly had no control over his own body as he lifted his hands and began to fire at the spider. The bullets hit in several places, little sprays of blood shooting out as it turned its pissed-off gaze on him.

He continued to fire against his will as it charged him. Charlotte and the others slipped through the door just as the spider lifted one of its good legs, cried out, and speared him through the chest.

CHAPTER SIX

As Charlotte and Cat scrutinized the stone archways cut into the chamber walls, her hope dwindled. They found no change in the opalescent substances filling the spaces between the archways. So far, her magic hadn't worked, and neither had other random ideas that had popped into her head. At that point, she was willing to try anything, and try anything she did.

She tested several of them by tossing smaller chunks of rock now littering the chamber's floor. Each piece of stone she hurled at the shimmering archways, whether lightly tossed or thrown with all her strength, gave no clues. The only results she found were disappointing at best.

Just as before, the ever-shifting, gelatinous substance that filled the archways put off glowing light. Every toss or throw she made resulted in the pebbles or larger rocks simply striking or even cracking against the substance before falling to the floor. It was as if she were throwing rocks at a solid brick wall.

Convinced the stones would offer no more clues, the fairy godmother turned to her magic again. Exploratory magic—spells used to read magical substances to discover what they might be made of or capable of—had no effect. She'd treated it like a science project since exploratory magic was like an experiment performed with a wand instead of the glass vials humans used across many worlds.

Deciding to move on to offensive magic to see if it sparked any reaction, she lifted her wand and widened her stance. The end of the wand glowed only moments before she aimed and flicked it at one of the archways.

Bolts of multicolored light streaked from the tip of her wand at one of her targets before she then aimed it at others. Growing frustrated, she cast every type of spell she could think of—light, heat, cold, spells to reveal the invisible, spells to compel other magic to submit to her commands, even literal activation spells.

None of these worked either.

After that, they dared to stand much closer to the shimmering archways than any reasonable being would consider safe. She'd thought that perhaps crowding the archways' personal space might activate one or two of them. She and Cat remained cautious and vigilant since the possible reactions were unknown and likely volatile, potentially containing threats like the wyrmling.

That produced the same results as all their other efforts.

Nothing.

Charlotte grew more frustrated before moving back to a safe distance, huffing, and dropping to the floor in defeat.

She scowled as she stared at the archways, her eyes slowly moving down the line to glare at each one.

"This is certainly not what I had in mind when I realized we needed to activate one of these damn things so we could continue forging ahead."

Charlotte sat roughly three meters away and facing the ninth archway. She had attempted to wake it up by coming within three inches of the shimmering opalescent substance. With her arms crossed over her chest and her wand sticking out from between two fingers of her right hand, Charlotte gritted her teeth.

With a sigh, she turned toward Cat. "Unfortunately, we're down to our last resort, which I didn't want to have to consider because it wasn't the most intelligent of things on our very limited list of options. However, those have been quickly dwindling for some time now anyway, and it appears we don't have another option. Safety is now out the window. It's either take a risk or remain trapped, and I don't plan to die in this cave.

"Alex is only safe if I'm alive. If I die, the magic surrounding him will break, and he'll simply stay in his current state. I suppose what happens to him then depends on the type of sleeping curse he's under. If it will hold him in total stasis like Aurora—rendering him immortal and eternally asleep until awoken—or if he would simply be in a deep sleep, which would mean he would slowly dehydrate and starve to death. We can't let that happen."

Cat shot her a quick glance, then sniffed at the tenth archway, which stood just a few feet to the right of the one she currently faced, as if he had found something new. The fairy godmother watched him intently, waiting for yet another sage bit of advice from a dog who couldn't actually speak.

To her horror, she watched with widening eyes as Cat's jaws opened and his tongue flicked out. Her immediate thought was that he meant to start licking the substance filling all the archways, but it was already too late. Before she could utter a pleading cry for him to stop, Cat's tongue slapped against the rock wall beside the stone archway, far enough away to avoid the magical goo.

"Oh, for the love of all things magical, Cat!" Charlotte scolded before she relaxed, sighed in relief, and rolled her eyes. "You have a special way of keeping me on my toes, don't you? I *really* thought for a minute you had abandoned that well-honed sense of reason I've seen you use plenty before." She paused as something occurred to her. "Wait a minute..."

Charlotte looked at Cat while he finished tasting the chamber wall, her eyes widening as he turned to look at her again.

"If you think for an instant I'm going to lick that wall, I suggest you start thinking of other options. And I strongly advise against you doing so too, no matter how fun it might seem to you right now." Her head fell back as she leaned back on her hands, frustrated as she began to speak while staring at the domed ceiling. "It seems our problem right now is that we haven't been reckless enough. We've been too careful, and it has used up quite enough of our precious time. We need to finish this quest and get back to Sir Thomas and Alex."

She groaned as she sat fully upright once again, looking toward the archway Cat stood next to. "Fine."

The fairy godmother stood and stretched, tilting her head from one side to the other to pop her aching neck. *I'm going to sleep for a month when all this is over, mark my words.*

After finally pulling his tongue off the smooth, circular wall beside the archway, Cat licked his muzzle several times and sneezed violently.

Charlotte approached the archway, her fingertips tingling in anticipation. Now that her arm was fully restored, she maintained a firm grip on her wand. With renewed determination and her mind firmly decided on a new approach, she almost wondered if the archway could sense her intentions as the opalescent sludge cast star-bursts into the corners of her eyes as if trying to distract her.

She took a deep breath, let it out in a quick, heavy sigh, and rolled her shoulders back. "Cat, if anything goes wrong, if you so much as *suspect* what you see doesn't look right, I'm counting on you to pull me back. Hopefully, it won't be another direct doorway into some terrible part of EverAfter that isn't where we need to be. However, if it gets this show on the road, I don't care what the hell it is. I just need to move forward. We can't be stuck in here forever." She paused and looked down at the large black dog. "You caught all that, right?"

She raised an eyebrow at her companion standing beside her. Cat's tail wagged vigorously, his midsection wobbling with the force, and his brown eyes darted between Charlotte's face and the shimmering archway.

She gave a curt nod. "Very well, then. I'll take that as a

yes. I'm going to assume you have given your word that you'll do everything in your power to yank me back if I make a potentially catastrophic mistake. This has to happen." She said that last bit more to herself than to Cat. "There's simply nothing left." With no other response from her companion, Charlotte returned her attention to the archway. "Here we go."

Holding her wand at the ready in her right hand, she reached out with her left toward the shimmering gelatinous wall. Throwing inanimate objects at it, hurling spells, and standing close enough to lick the sludge herself if she'd chosen to do so had all been futile. Perhaps the archways needed more than pebbles and generic magic to open them.

Maybe they needed Charlotte specifically, or even Cat, but she wasn't desperate enough to test her theory on him.

"Get ready for it," she whispered, unsure whether she meant it more for herself or Cat. Then she bit the proverbial bullet and pushed her hand forward.

The tips of Charlotte's index and middle fingers first brushed the opalescent sludge, and she paused, waiting to see if anything would happen with such a light touch. There was such a thing as going too far too quickly, of course, and she wouldn't make that mistake again.

However, the only response she got was a warm, tingling energy snaking up her arm. No pain, no shock, nothing worthy of a warning to leave the archway alone. Swallowing nervously, she reached farther and pushed the rest of her fingers deeper into the sludge. It felt like a mix of warm mud and cool water enveloping them. It was a strange sensation.

Unfortunately, what she didn't expect to find was the cold, solid surface of stone behind the unknown substance.

"Damn it!" she snapped, pulling her hand back and placing both hands on her hips. She stared, fuming for several moments as her chest rose and fell rapidly with every quick breath. Finally, she shook her head and gave it another go. "No. That can't be it. That doesn't help us at all, and I refuse to believe we were just shut in here for no damn reason."

Charlotte pushed a bit more, hoping her anger and determination would be enough to spark something, but the stone was completely solid and unyielding.

"Fine!" She pulled her hand away and looked down at her fingers, now coated with an inch and a half of the opalescent slime. Her nose wrinkled as she looked down at the side of her dress that had a large streak of it. She groaned and rolled her eyes. "Lovely."

Not that it matters much after the large tear and blood stain ruined it.

She flicked the goop away from the material and did the same with the rest of what remained on her fingers, sending it splattering across the stone floor beside her before focusing back on the problem at hand.

"Now what?"

Cat didn't have an answer, and neither did Charlotte now that their last resort seemed spent.

She looked down at her fingers. Though the sludge no longer covered them, they were still a bit wet, which did little beyond providing a brief chill when she moved her hand through the air. Even the short-lived tingle had disappeared.

"Well, now I'm entirely out of ideas, Cat. If you have any brilliant last-minute long shots that might get us some kind of response out of this place, do speak now or forever hold your peace." When Cat gave no reply, she found herself sighing yet again. If there was an award for most sighs in a single day, she briefly thought she'd have won it by now. "Honestly, what does a fairy godmother have to do around here to get a little—"

A furious tremble racked the chamber, cutting her off. The stone floor bucked and jerked, sending Charlotte to her hands and knees while Cat splayed his feet further apart and whined. The cavern seemed like some ancient beast awakening for the first time in eons. The floor rocked and shuddered, sending tremors up the walls and across the domed ceiling. Several more large chunks of the ceiling split away from the now widening cracks the wyrmling's head had left earlier.

Cat barked once and crawled toward the sludge on the floor that Charlotte had flicked off her fingers, sniffing at it intently.

Charlotte tried to stand to get to a safer place by the walls, but she only fell once again. Doing so allowed her to realize the safest spot appeared to be the center of the chamber.

"Cat, leave it!" she shouted over the strengthening roar in her ears.

If I'd known swiping that junk all over the ground would cause a reaction, I would have done it far sooner.

Charlotte jolted as another chunk of stone fell from the ceiling and crashed dangerously close to her and Cat, who quickly stumbled his way over to her. Afraid this would get worse before it got better, Charlotte flicked her wand to erect a brilliant silver shield around them. Another rock fell and bounced off her magic before shattering into pieces on the ground. Charlotte stared down at Cat with wide eyes.

"So, this is great! I succeeded in bringing this whole place down around our heads, is that it? Gods! This is *not* what I meant when I said we needed to exhaust all our options. I don't think I can blast my way through this."

Cat met her stare as another earthquake threw everything into violent chaos. The tremor only lasted around fifteen seconds, though it felt more like fifteen minutes as more chunks of falling stone fell around Charlotte and Cat and straight down on top of the barrier.

Despite her shield, she and Cat did their best to crawl out of the direct path of the worst damage to avoid any potential harm if the barrier were to break. It was better to stay agile than rely solely on the shield, especially when magic had been unreliable for the last two months. On a quest like this, there was no telling when fate would decide to snatch practical and reliable magic away from her yet again.

By the time the earthquake finally stopped, Charlotte and Cat had scrambled back to the center of the circular chamber. It seemed safer there, since there was more space above them to notice if the ceiling broke away and more distance between them and the dozens of glowing archways lining the chamber's perimeter.

As the tremors faded, the two adventurers stayed perfectly still, watching their surroundings and nearly holding their breaths in anticipation.

"Oh, come on!" Charlotte barked, turning slowly to inspect the various archways, seeing no change.

Rage started to well in her, and she suddenly felt the urge to abandon the whole thing, get Alex and Sir Thomas, and just blast their way out. Damn the consequences. Damn the quest. Someone *else* could save the day for once. She was tired, and she'd had all the fun from the festivities she could handle and wanted to get out and go home.

Her eyes skipped from one door to another again before she slumped in defeat, falling on her hip into a resting position. "What the hell does this even mean? There's no such thing as coincidence. I just stuck my fingers into a magical substance I don't recognize, flicked it on the ground, and all of that only a *moment* before another earthquake hit this quest cave? You can't tell me that doesn't mean anything, right?"

She quickly glanced at Cat, but he did nothing more than let his tongue fall from the side of his mouth as he panted. There was no usual bark or yip in response. Instead, he remained relatively still beside the fairy godmother under the protection of her silvery dome.

Suddenly, his ears perked up and swiveled in short, twitchy movements as he panted and scanned the chamber. This time, he didn't look at Charlotte, which set off alarm bells in her mind.

"What is it? Do you hear or smell something? Is there another threat on the way?" Irritation bubbled up in her chest. "I *wish* I could talk with you like Sir Thomas does. This would be so much easier! Can you tell me *anything?*" When he didn't respond right away, she felt her resolve slip entirely. "Cat! Focus! What do y—"

Another deafening rumble cut through Charlotte's words, and her body stiffened as she rose to her knees, fully alert. This time, the rumbling didn't come with the physical tremor through the stone floor. It wasn't another earthquake.

Something was happening within the chamber.

CHAPTER SEVEN

Cat barked wildly just before another tremble ripped through the chamber where he and Charlotte sat huddled together under the barrier. The tremor didn't come from the floor or deep underground, which would have signified another earthquake. Instead, the roaring sound came from the walls of the chamber.

By the time the fairy godmother pieced together where the disturbance was coming from, the circular walls had already begun to move.

Her eyes widened, and her jaw fell slightly open as her head moved on a swivel. Resting on all fours to maintain her balance, she quickly glanced all around the room, her heart racing as she watched the chamber change before her very eyes.

"What's happening?" she cried out, even knowing Catt wouldn't have an answer any more than she did.

Charlotte could barely hear her own voice over the grumbling roar of the stone walls grinding and moving against the stone ceiling and floor where they connected.

Cat's non-stop barking didn't help matters. Whether he was warning her to prepare for what was to come next or lashing out at the unknown event happening in the chamber itself, Charlotte had no idea. All she could do was stay and wait in the center with Cat at her side as they helplessly watched the dozens of glowing opalescent archways around them spin clockwise with increasing speed.

Tremors from the grinding stone traveled through the floor and vibrated her body. She clenched her jaw to keep her teeth from chattering as the sound in the room grew worse as the speed increased.

"Cat! Cover your ears!" she called out before shoving down between his shoulder blades until he went prone.

He put his lower forelegs over his ears, pinching them closed as tightly as he could manage while Charlotte stayed on her knees and doubled over before placing her hands tightly over hers. She wished she could help Cat more, but she was so distracted that casting a spell in such unstable conditions could cause more harm than good. She took solace in knowing she could heal Cat if the worst were to happen, and she hoped he felt confident with that as well.

It occurred to her that it was possible it was the floor moving and not the walls. It would have made more sense, but aside from tremors, she felt no movement. If the floor *was* moving, with them being in the center, she wasn't sure if that would cause her to feel it more or less than if they were closer to the walls.

Cat howled, and her chest clenched. She had no way of discerning if it was out of pain, fear, something else entirely, or a mix of everything.

The walls kept spinning, and splinters of colorful,

refracted light glinted across the floor, flashing off Charlotte's dark purple cloak and Cat's pitch-black fur. The noise grew almost unbearably loud, even with them covering their ears, and Charlotte thought she would have to take the risk of attempting a spell to keep their heads from exploding. A headache had already begun to split her skull, and she couldn't even imagine what poor Cat was experiencing.

"That's it," she ground out, though she may as well have said nothing for the lack of sound it made against the roar of the magical room.

She rose, crying out in terrible pain as she pulled her wand hand away from her ear. Without hesitation, she lifted her wand shakily as she silently prayed for a positive outcome. Then, near-complete silence fell over them as the shifting walls ground to a halt.

Charlotte's eyes were wide as she stayed completely still, frozen where she knelt, one hand over her left ear and her wand hand raised. The faintest glow came from the tip because she was only part of the way through charging it when everything stopped.

Without moving her body, her eyes darted back and forth, studying their surroundings as she waited for something awful to begin again. When she was satisfied for the moment, she slowly began to lower her hands, and she turned her attention to Cat.

Low whines cut through the near silence; the only other sound in the chamber was the tiny clicks and taps of dust and other small debris settling into their new positions.

Charlotte dove forward and pulled Cat's forearms away

from his ears. She lifted her wand, using it to create a light that allowed her to see better. The fairy godmother lifted the possibly wounded ears and peered inside. There was no blood, and from what she could tell, no visible damage, but inflammation had already begun, which meant *something* had happened she couldn't see.

"It's okay, Cat. Can you hear me?" He whined in response, and she sighed in relief as she leaned over and kissed the top of his head. "Are you still in pain?" He whined again, and she lifted herself away from him. "Okay, buddy. I'm going to fix you up. Remember, this could hurt, and I'm so sorry if it does."

He whined and let out a soft yip before lifting his head enough to lick her hand. She smiled softly.

"You're such a good boy, Cat. I'll take that as a yes to continue, right?"

He licked her again, and her chest tightened. She pulled his front half into her lap to hold him tightly so he could feel safer while she healed him. Luckily, whatever the damage was, it obviously wasn't terrible, which likely meant healing would move quickly. Like her, he might have had a splitting headache instead of any actual damage. She wasn't exactly vet material, so she had no way of knowing without being able to speak to Cat and receive answers in return.

As she raised her wand, the tip began to glow, and Cat shifted in her lap, though he didn't whine. She hoped that meant he wasn't in pain. As she cast the spell, warmth filled her as well, and she realized she'd put a bit more into it than she imagined.

The warmth traveled up her body and into her head, instantly soothing her head.

Did I somehow cast that on myself and not Cat?

Suddenly, the light at the tip of the wand snuffed out, and Cat darted to his feet before tackling her to the ground and licking all over her face as he gave happy-sounding whines.

She laughed freely as she wrapped her arms around the big, clumsy dog, realizing she'd cast the spell on them both. She'd felt no pain, and Cat never whined once, so she imagined he felt nothing either, which made her feel incredibly grateful.

Maybe headaches are different than actual ailments, she thought as she had to shove Cat back forcibly.

"You're welcome, Cat," she said, still giggling as she rose again to a sitting position. "I'm so glad you feel better. Did the spell cause you pain?" He snorted with a quick side-to-side jerk of his head, and she smiled. "I'm so glad."

Using her cloak, she wiped away the layer of dog slobber she had all over her face. She didn't mind Cat's kisses, but she drew the limit at slobbering on her face, though she'd never tell him that.

"I guess it's time to get back to work," she said as she cautiously climbed to her feet. She was almost afraid to let the magic of the barrier go, so she kept it for the time being.

For several seconds, Charlotte warily eyed the rest of the chamber.

"I don't know if that last earthquake brought us a surprise or if me touching that substance or flicking it to the floor set something off. Cat, what do you think?"

He lowered himself into a defensive crouch as he scanned the chamber like a sentinel.

"I'm right there with you. I still don't know yet if this is a good sign, but without knowing what we're to face next, we have no idea what to prepare for."

She watched Cat from the corner of her eye. He became increasingly agitated. She had only seen him this defensively aggressive once or twice before, usually right before stepping into highly dangerous territory. She couldn't ignore his reactions. He was, after all, exceptional.

Just as she finished her thought, Cat whirled around to face the other side of the chamber, his hackles raised and his tail sticking straight out.

"All right, Cat, I'm listening. What do you sense in here? Because if we have to fight another wyrmling back through an open doorway into EverAfter, I might start to think we've been led disastrously astray on this quest."

She turned to face the direction of Cat's new target and searched the archways on the other side of the chamber. It didn't take long for her to see what had caught her companion's attention.

"Oh, damn. That can't be good."

The first archway she noticed shimmered with a pearly light before filling it with blurry dark shapes that were similar to those she saw in the wyrmling's archway. The light flashed brighter, and the shapes began to darken, shifting and merging into familiar images.

Seconds later, Charlotte recognized the scene within the archway as the ancient forest where she, Alex, Sir Thomas, and Cat had found themselves after surviving the magical storm and earthquake. That forest was no longer the land behind Ginger Haus's suburban neighborhood but was instead filled with enormous old trees and damp moss.

"Seems to me this place is offering us a quick and easy way out of here. I suppose if I were a more selfish fairy godmother who only cared about her own safety, I would definitely take it. However, I'm absolutely *not* selfish, and I would never leave anyone behind. Even if it meant I was stuck in here forever."

A low, warning snarl came from Cat at her side, and she turned to face the other archways only to discover each filling with their own images and landscapes. At first, they were blurry and dark, but they soon cleared to provide doorway-sized glimpses into other realms.

Charlotte quickly realized how vastly different each of these archways were. She caught sight of the thick forest of her home in EverAfter, the trees old and wise, though not as dark and ominous as the sacred woods where she and her companions had found the cave entrance. The woods in this archway were undoubtedly those of the enchanted forest of EverAfter, where many stories had become legends.

She then saw the familiar streets, shops, and market-places of Prince Charming's kingdom, with a glimpse of his castle in the distance. Other arches revealed fields, valleys, villages, and darkened castles belonging to both villains and heroes. But it wasn't only the known landmarks of EverAfter that caught the fairy godmother's eye. In fact, those were practically boring compared to some of the other images.

One such view within a glowing stone archway revealed a castle made of transparent green sea glass. Its spires rose from an ocean floor amid tall, wavering forests of kelp and vibrant strands of coral. Sunlight glinted through the water, casting shimmering ripples against the castle walls and sandy courtyards, while schools of fish in various shapes, sizes, and bright colors flitted among them. If Charlotte had not already been certain of what she was looking at, the merfolk going about their business in their underwater kingdom would have confirmed it.

Another archway offered a view into a fiery hellscape of jagged crags and skies blackened by smoke and soot, with bursts of fire shooting up from fissures in the earth.

A different doorway showed the island of Neverland. At the same time, another hosted several ships captained by both recognized owners and self-proclaimed pirates, all moored at the docks of a bustling, stinking shipyard city on the coast. Yet another doorway revealed a pixie nest, and another centered upon impossibly tall cliffs where dragons and their riders made their homes.

Everywhere Charlotte looked, stone archways opened into shimmering images of other magical worlds. Most she recognized, but she found one that made no sense. It was a glittering cityscape, bigger and more vibrant than Cincinnati and seemingly fueled by neon lights and enormous cars racing through the air.

She suddenly felt remarkably out of place. Even as an adventurer explicitly chosen for this quest to find answers for both EverAfter and Alex's human world. Charlotte was uncertain she could handle the realization that there were even more worlds beyond those she had known.

The Fairy Godmothers' Guild had long been aware of Earth as a world without magic, inhabited by humans. As far as Charlotte knew, this awareness was purely intellectual. Now, however, she realized the Guild might have conspired in various ways for their own self-interest.

After all, it would be next to impossible to find your way back to EverAfter—and therefore back to the people who you could tell about what the Guild had done to you—if you were unable to use magic of any kind because they banished you to a land without magic. She had never heard of any EverAfteran visiting Earth for recreational travel. Those who had gone were *supposed* to be no one other than villains who had been banished through the portal.

Though her group now knew it wasn't only the villains after all but innocents, too.

Charlotte couldn't help but wonder what all these doors into different realms had to do with her quest. As she slowly spun in the center of the chamber, she saw another world revealed within a glowing doorway.

It was Cincinnati.

Charlotte recognized it instantly. There was the Roebling Bridge and the dome of the Carew Tower. She had visited both, sometimes with Alex by her side. Among the views of enchanted forests, magical lakes, rural villages, castles, and hellscapes, the unexpected sight of Cincinnati, Ohio stuck out like a sore thumb.

Despite the inconvenience of being tossed into Cincinnati and left to fend for herself without magic, Charlotte had come to think of the city as a second home over the past two months. She had grown to respect and even care for its people, places, and landmarks. The city held a small but fond place in her heart because it had led her to unexpected and wonderful discoveries.

Even amidst her banishment, which she now knew was likely orchestrated by her own Fairy Godmothers' Guild.

But seeing it here amidst all these other magical worlds...

"This is incredible," she breathed.

If Cincinnati has been connected to these realms from the very beginning, then the Guild knew far more about the human world than they ever taught me or my sister godmothers. They've been keeping this whole thing secret from us for millennia.

If that were the case, Ginger Haus's warning about the Guild and the massive conspiracy from Charlotte's own superiors seemed even more plausible, and Charlotte Weaver had been caught in the middle of it.

She'd come to believe that theory in the weeks following their time at Ginger's cottage, but this was completely different. There was a significant difference between coming to a basic understanding that you still had to work through and process and being smacked in the face with the truth.

And right here it was. What more proof could she need? Her mind reeled as one question after another darted through her mind. The moment one skipped through, another came through right after.

Is part of my quest to discover how false my own Guild, superiors, and mentors have been for thousands of years? Or that Cincinnati is more special in the realm of legends than anyone has given it credit for? What am I supposed to do with all this? If I'm the only fairy godmother here, then I'm likely the only fairy godmother outside of the superiors who know. It would be nearly impossible to get anyone else to listen to me and believe something I'm still having a hard time coming to grips with.

Charlotte looked down at Cat, who stood beside her, scanning the entire chamber intently for any potential threats.

"This will sound like a stupid question, but you *do* see all this, right? All these different worlds, all these different types of people and creatures." He glanced at her briefly before giving a soft *roo* in response, and she let out a heavy breath. "Some of these, I... I've never seen them before in my life, and that's saying something. I've been nearly everywhere. Well, I *thought* I had." She scoffed lightly in disbelief. "Apparently, there is a lot I don't know. A lot no one ever told me. All of which I now find to be *very* suspicious."

The longer she and her companion stood there, gazing at the different realms through the doorways, the greater the sense of urgency filling Charlotte's awareness grew. This was a remarkable find, a sight most people—even most fairy godmothers—could only dream of encountering. Here she was, standing in the center of an enormous portal room with open doorways leading to dozens of other worlds, many of which she neither recognized nor could name.

"All right then," she said, nodding curtly and looking for an archway that felt like the most appropriate place to start. "If the cavern has offered us all these doors, this is obviously the next part of our quest. One of them is bound to be exactly where we're supposed to end up. The question is, is there a specific order, or do we test until we find the correct one?"

Cat let out a low chuff, swinging his head back and forth to eye one archway after another. Charlotte couldn't decide on one that looked the best either, so she shrugged.

"Actually, you know what? Why don't you go ahead and pick the first one? I trust your judgment. It seems you are more than a cat who was transformed into a dog. Your senses and understanding of all things magical are quite unmatched. You've saved my behind more than a few times. Besides, I think I may be experiencing something like decision anxiety for the first time. I'm sure it will work itself out eventually, but you should definitely pick first. You select our next destination, and I will follow you all the way to the end."

Cat looked at her, the reflections of so many glowing archways filled with shadows, shapes, and creatures all reflected in his eyes. Another sharp yip told the fairy godmother all she needed to know just a moment before he started toward one of the archways.

If I told this to any other fairy godmother in the Guild, they would tell me I was crazy for leaving this up to a street cat I accidentally enchanted into a dog. But they don't know Cat, do they? And he has never steered me wrong.

Not once.

CHAPTER EIGHT

"Nope. Uh-uh. Absolutely not." Sir Thomas folded his arms and shook his head, trying to appear committed and confident. "I intend to sit here until Lady Charlotte and Cat return, and I highly doubt anything has the power to change my mind."

However, something did have that power.

The more minor, frequent earthquakes that had shaken the cavern during Charlotte and Cat's absence had grown in frequency, and Sir Thomas' misgivings had grown alongside them.

He had counted four so far, though there might have been one or two he missed while focusing on Detective Taylor's safety. For the most part, he felt confident in his ability to track the earthquakes, but he noted more and more each time how they steadily eroded his confidence in Lady Charlotte's plans.

It didn't help that another archway had appeared in the chamber, one that hadn't been there before. If that wasn't a direct order from the quest cave to continue, he didn't know what was.

Sir Thomas couldn't help but glance at it repeatedly, whether during the tremors or in the calm that followed. Still, he forced his attention back to Detective Taylor, hoping to see some sign that the unknown ailment was nearing its end.

Unfortunately, Alex's condition remained unchanged. Just as before, he continued to lay within the silvery-white protective magic, still hovering three feet above the cavern floor.

When the earthquakes started again, there was no indication that the detective was aware of them or could respond to the impending dangers. This was the main reason Charlotte and her companions had headed to the woods in the first place: to find the source of the earthquakes and stop them.

However, the tremors within the cavern only worsened over time, and Sir Thomas began to wonder if this was related to their party accepting the quest and entering the cave. He could have pondered these questions until Charlotte and Cat returned from their journey deeper into the cave, and he'd undoubtedly planned to, but he lost that opportunity as another quake rocked the area surrounding him and Alex.

This one was vastly more powerful than the last few, with more drastic effects on the cavern itself. The chamber began to show signs of buckling under the increasingly violent tremors. Sir Thomas was concerned that he lacked the skills to consistently dodge the large chunks of stone and earth falling from the ceiling and walls. As a cat, he was incredibly agile, and he was sure he could dodge them on his own...

But he wasn't on his own.

And Alex was in his care and under his protection.

Most of these chunks were nearly on top of him and Detective Taylor before he could see them, making his responsibilities that much more difficult.

The worst was yet to come, and he briefly wondered if this was the quest cave's way of *forcing* him through the new door.

Oncoming tremors of yet another earthquake interrupted Sir Thomas' thoughts, distracting him before he had an opportunity to assess the state of the cavern and attempt to avoid the falling debris. Two enormous chunks of stone plummeting from the darkness above nearly smashed Sir Thomas between them.

They collided with the floor much closer to his position than he'd anticipated, and both hit at nearly the same time, leaving him no room to leap to the left or right. The cavern wall was directly in front of him, and he assumed that would be a safer place to shelter, but with such a significant threat at that moment, his only option was to leap backward as far and as fast as possible to avoid being crushed.

His back thumped into something warm and solid that instantly gave beneath his weight, and he cried out in surprise before realizing what it was. Then he cried out in horror and scrambled to regain his balance before spinning around.

"Oh, Detective! I'm so sorry. Are you alright? Are you hurt? Did I—"

He stopped immediately when he caught sight of Detective Taylor, realizing the human was not where Sir Thomas had left him. Bits and pieces of the cavern dropped all around them, crashing onto the ground with earsplitting cracks and thunderous booms that added to the reverberating roar of the earthquake.

Sir Thomas could only stare in mute horror at the prone human wrapped in silvery white light, gliding across the enormous cavern as if on an invisible conveyor belt, drawn to its next station. He immediately thought of earlier when he'd moved on his own, and he got chills now, realizing that likely wasn't a coincidence.

Before Charlotte had left, there had been a magical tether that connected Alex to her, allowing her to move and pull him along. When she'd crossed through to the next part of her journey, that tether was severed, leaving the protection spell active.

This, however, was different.

There was no tether, no conveyor belt, and no one waited on the other side of the detective's trajectory to stop him or guide him to safety. And all while the sleep-cursed human seemingly roamed free, the cavern continued to crumble around them.

"What is happening?" The horrified question emerged from Sir Thomas' lips in a breathless whisper.

His eyes darted around the cavern, from the enormous falling chunks of stone to the silvery magic surrounding Detective Taylor, who floated quickly across the space while narrowly avoiding the falling debris and resulting enormous cracks fracturing the stone floor.

Thanks to Charlotte's magic, the light surrounding Alex

made him almost appear heroic as he sailed away from Sir Thomas.

For a moment, the talking cat was unable to move, paralyzed by his fear of the stones dropping around him and the sight of his unconscious human companion miraculously skirting past all the danger without a scratch.

Something must *be steering him because no one can be* that *lucky,* he thought.

Still, he was certain Detective Taylor's luck could only hold so long, regardless of whether something—or some*one*—was steering him or if it was a random freak occurrence.

With an exasperated sigh, Sir Thomas scanned the falling stones around him, gauged his timing, and raced after the steadily floating human. "I'm coming, Detective!"

He dodged another boulder before leaping and twisting midair to avoid the shards ricocheting off the cavern floor. It was as if the place had taken his presence as a personal insult, and the debris was out for blood.

Sir Thomas managed to avoid the worst of it, catching only a few pebbles that bounced off his hat and thick coat. His fur provided enough padding to keep away the worst of the damage, and he shook it off with a quick twitch from head to tail before leaping back into action.

With little time to spare, he closed the distance between himself and Alex. The earthquake had finally ceased for now, but the damage to the cavern walls and ceiling continued. Just as Sir Thomas was about to reach the human in his care, a deafening crack split the air. Another enormous hunk of rock plummeted out of the darkness, narrowly missing the bobbing globe of light Charlotte had left behind.

Sir Thomas saw Alex still sailing smoothly away from him despite how much closer he had come. With feline swiftness, he judged the distance, speeds, and trajectories of all three moving forces: the falling rock, the floating detective, and himself.

Without further thought, Sir Thomas darted into a dead run toward the detective, letting loose a trembling battle cry that would have terrified even seasoned warriors if they could have heard it over the crashing roar and destruction around him.

A falling rock headed straight toward Detective Taylor. Sir Thomas couldn't say how protective Charlotte's magic truly was, and he wasn't about to take a chance that anything could push through it as he'd done earlier when messing with Alex's hair.

Dodging around smaller bits of falling ceiling and cavern wall, he managed a daring leap onto one such falling stone, using it as leverage to throw himself toward the calculated point of impact.

His warbling cry cut through the air again. With both paws extended in front of him, Sir Thomas connected with the magical case surrounding Alex, shoving him hard forward only a heartbeat before the talking cat hit the floor and tumbled over several times.

A deafening *crack* like shattering bones split the air only a few feet behind Sir Thomas, bouncing him in the air for a moment as shrapnel from the rock exploded in every direction. Several larger chunks hit the wide brim of his hat, which he'd only barely kept hold of, and at least one piece of rubble struck him in the shoulder.

Groaning, he brought himself to a sitting position and rotated his arm. It hurt like hell, but he didn't think it was broken. He was just grateful it hadn't been his sword arm. Alex's predicament soon entered his mind, and Sir Thomas audibly gasped as he remembered he had a detective to catch.

With no time to lose, Sir Thomas leaped up and spun around to face Alex, sparing a quick glance at the shattered rock pieces that had once been the massive falling boulder he'd saved his companion from only moments before. He hurried after Alex, running as fast as he could until he got within a comfortable distance.

With a grunt and a final leap, he landed with both paws clamped onto the detective's shoulders. The fairy godmother's protective magic offered no resistance to his touch, and he once again wondered if that meant other things could make it through. Finally, he gained control of his unconscious charge amidst the danger crashing down around them.

"I've got you, Detective," he said breathlessly, pulling Alex's floating form to a stop.

He'd expected to feel some resistance, as if something *had* been pulling him along, but he felt nothing so far. However, that still didn't convince him the cave or something in it didn't have a hold on the human.

"Not to fear. That was a close one, but we made it through. I think the earthquake has finally passed, and the worst of the chaos in this cavern has died down."

Until the next tremor races through this place. Then we'll be forced to do this all over again. I'm not sure how much longer I can manage any of this.

As suddenly as the last earthquake had begun, the aftermath dimmed to nothing more than a few smaller stones and pebbles clacking against the floor. Enormous piles of fallen rubble littered the once clear cavern floor, but that was hardly an obstacle for Sir Thomas. He could move quickly and gracefully across all terrains, and for now, Detective Taylor didn't even need to touch the ground.

The real trouble now was figuring out how much longer they would have to remain vigilant during the earthquakes plaguing the cavern and perhaps the rest of the quest cave. Sir Thomas hoped that wherever Lady Charlotte and Cat were, they would be safely away from the bulk of the earthquakes' effects. Something told him that if they'd felt these tremors here as well as in Cincinnati, the magical interference they'd hypothesized might have come from this place all along.

We may have come to the wrong conclusion entirely about all of this. And if that's the case, I fear for what Lady Charlotte and Cat are currently experiencing.

The overwhelming silence in the cavern hadn't lasted more than a few minutes before it was broken by a sound that Sir Thomas once again thought he was imagining.

"Sir Thomas? Sir Thomas, are you there? Can you hear me?"

CHAPTER NINE

"I wish you could tell me exactly why you picked this one first," Charlotte said, folding her arms as she stopped behind Cat.

The Newfoundland had led her to what he presumably deemed the safest option after the chamber had stopped spinning, revealing the shimmering opalescent archways had solidified into individual doors to different realms.

"Then I might have an easier time understanding how your decision-making process operates. Because, as it stands right now, I honestly can't fathom what was going through your mind."

Cat turned away from the open archway and panted, his tongue lolling out.

"This is Swamp Rat territory, Cat," Charlotte explained with a hint of exasperation as she gestured toward the image of a murky swamp that glowed faintly within the stone archway.

She started to wonder if she'd thought too soon when

trusting Cat's judgment, thinking that he'd never led her astray before.

"In case you haven't figured it out by now, that includes all the enormous rats and their various cousins who call this place home."

Her eyes narrowed as she stared into his large, innocent brown eyes. *I wish I knew what was going on in that head, Cat, because from the looks of it, it isn't much.*

"You do understand that, right? Surely, it isn't a good idea for us to walk through a portal that's more likely to get us sucked down into the mud and eaten alive than to help us find our way back to the right path on this quest. I *really* feel like we need to move to something else."

Cat barked in disagreement, but the fairy godmother's worry grew by the second. He'd been right about everything so far, but *swamp rat territory?* She couldn't understand that at all.

"I'm sure you have excellent reasons for picking this first, but I'm in no hurry to be buried alive, eaten, torn apart, drowned, or any of the other many, *many* deadly possibilities that could happen in a place like that, especially when we don't know how these portals work. The wyrmling was able to fly right through, seemingly without any negative side effects. Then again, that same wyrmling also gave itself a concussion against the ceiling, so my level of confidence is still a bit lacking at this point."

Cat continued to walk across the chamber with Charlotte, eyeing the different glowing windows of light and searching for one that might aid them in their quest. Some of the portal images within the stone terrified Charlotte, causing her to glance at them only briefly before moving on.

One archway seemed to contain ghosts, another held a half-man, half-monster creature, and a third resembled EverAfter or even Earth, with human-like figures crossing in front of the archway. However, a shudder ran through Charlotte when she realized the denizens had humanoid bodies, but perfectly square, shiny silver heads made of reflective metal.

That was not a world she wished to visit. Not now, not *ever*, but especially not during their quest.

After following Cat to nearly a dozen archways and rejecting his choices each time, Charlotte had to stop. She knew what she'd told Cat, and she'd meant it, but all this just felt...*wrong*.

"I'm sorry, Cat. Wait just a sec," she panted, doubling over and propping herself up with her hands on her thighs. "For some reason, I'm *exhausted*. Probably all the energy it took to heal myself earlier still messing with me. I never used a rejuvenation spell and used quite a bit more magic after."

She paused for several moments, trying to gather herself so she could continue.

"Hopefully, this feeling will go away soon, but I can't say. I never expected this level of exertion without much to show for it. Adrenaline probably played a part in keeping me alert for a while as well. Then again, knowing that we aren't even close to finished here really makes me feel my age right now, and that definitely isn't helping." She sighed.

After laying it all out there on the table for her furry companion to assess, Charlotte looked at Cat and couldn't help but huff out a wry laugh. "Actually, now that I'm keeled over—half dying from walking around a room—I think I've been deluding myself."

Cat tilted his head curiously to the side, urging her to continue.

"My magic is operating with full force again, and it works *exactly* the way it's supposed to. It's been *months* since we arrived in Cincinnati, and my magic has never worked right the entire time. It takes years, *decades*, to train to the level I was at because magic pulls from the user's energy. I haven't used this kind of power in months." She shook her head and sighed. "I'm weak. That's all there is to it. *That's* why I feel so awful. Despite it not being by choice, my body and capabilities grew weaker, and I'm having a hard time with this quest because of it."

The giant black Newfoundland snorted and gave a rough shake of his head before wagging his tail. She smiled.

"Thanks for your vote of confidence, my furry friend, but simply put, I'm out of shape. Magically speaking."

Grimacing, she gingerly reached out to rub the lower portion of her rib cage where she had healed a gash. Apparently, it took either a more potent spell or far more rest than she had given herself to thoroughly heal the underlying damage that had not been immediately visible through the rip in her dress.

It felt like she'd healed the most dangerous parts, which was anything cut open that risked infection, but now she was left feeling like a mule had kicked her in the side. Charlotte wondered if she and Cat were ever going to make it out of there.

I feel like I've missed something vital and, more than likely, very obvious.

She gave herself a moment to gather her energy and senses, then stood upright and nodded at Cat. "All right, let's try it one more time. We'll look at another archway and see if any of them are viable options for us to move through. I don't like the idea of portal hopping, especially with Sir Thomas and Alex still behind in that first cavern, but there might not be another choice."

Her eyes wandered around the cavern. "Nothing we've accomplished in this room has been of any real benefit. I thought quest caves and their secrets were supposed to be navigable by those who are worthy of said quest. Well, unless that was another lie."

The other possibility was that something was inherently wrong with the quest cave. Perhaps the earthquakes, which had reached all the way here from Cincinnati, had affected it. Maybe there was another magical interference causing both the earthquakes and this revolving room full of portals to malfunction.

When she focused on the archways again, Charlotte's attention zeroed in on the second closest shimmering doorway. She took a step toward it and pointed. "What about that one? A sleepy-looking village with nothing but farmers doesn't make for the most exciting destination, but if we need to escape this chamber by moving through one of these archways, I'm inclined to pick the most harmless exit. What do you think?"

Of course, the first archway—the one with a focused image of a sprawling valley at the base of the mountains and *The Castle on the Hill* rising in the distance—had seemed harmless enough but was anything but.

The wyrmling had appeared seemingly out of nowhere and raced into the chamber at the last second to gorge itself on the presumably easy prey standing there. Charlotte could no more predict which of these archways was safer or more dangerous than she could unravel all the other mysteries of this place. She was still trying to figure out precisely what they were looking for and what they needed to do to overcome the obstacles facing them now.

"Why not try it, hmm?" she mused, sounding far more confident of the idea than she felt. "What's the worst that could happen? We find something we don't like and have to come hauling ass back through? I mean, that sounds like plenty of the other adventures we've had in the last few months. Nothing we can't handle, right?"

She quickly approached the archway with the sleepy-looking village centered in its shimmering view. Behind her, Cat remained motionless and silent.

"This could be another trick of this chamber," she thought aloud before cursing under her breath. "I'm sure most adventurers choose the far more harrowing and deadly path. That's exactly what I would expect a hero to do. I don't think taking the easy road and heading back to a harmless farming village garners the same honor and awe as walking through a portal into a dragon's lair. Perhaps all we need to do is choose the safer course, the more predictable one."

Charlotte paused a foot away from the village archway, then snorted. "Trying to figure all this out is worse than trying to help Alex figure out some of those awful cases he comes home with. He always says the most obvious answer is usually the right one, but I don't think that theory works in quests or quest caves. Because instinct tells me to start small and only go harder and more dangerous if necessary. That makes sense to me logically, but experience from EverAfter tells me that courageous heroes on a magical quest to save two worlds would choose something dangerous and worthy of a test. However, if we fail–"

She trailed off, leaving the truth hanging in the air in silence rather than speaking aloud what they both already knew.

If we fail, Alex and Sir Thomas will likely die in here.

Despite her words, Charlotte wasn't reassured about her choices. That didn't stop her from reaching toward the shimmering portal showing a village. "It seemed easy enough for the wyrmling. Just push straight on through, right? Can't be that hard if our hungry flying friend managed to do it in the blink of an eye."

She didn't wait for Cat to respond before reaching toward the image of the small, rural village with its freshly cut timber fences and open pastures dotted with livestock and other creatures grazing on the lush grasses.

"This one does look simple and nice," she murmured.

But when her fingertips grazed the shimmering light of the archway's window—what should have been a portal— her fingers were stopped by the cold, hard stone on the other side. There was no sludge this time, just a natural resistance preventing her from moving through any further.

Charlotte had no choice but to withdraw her hand and glower at the image of the sleepy village with a growl.

"Bullshit," she cursed at the archway. "This frickin' cave is hardly playing fair. What even is this? Wyrmlings can pass through without difficulty, but a fairy godmother can't get her hand two inches into a different realm? That doesn't make any sense. I'm a magical being, and I should be able to cross if I want to. That wyrmling never should have been able to breach it in the first place."

"While there is little that truly pisses me off, these puzzles leading to nowhere are doing a *fine* job. There may be no way out of this place, and we wouldn't know because none of the traditional rules apply. What is going on here? I'm honestly at the end of my—"

Cat interrupted her with a bark filled with warning, aggression, and a hint of fear. It sounded different from his previous warnings.

Despite hearing no verbal words, she somehow understood him with perfect clarity: *Get ready. This is going to be a big one.*

Charlotte's eyes widened as they snapped over to Cat in shock. "Wait, what? Did I just—"

Something rattled in the direction Cat was facing, and she spun to see whatever had alarmed him. While Charlotte desperately wanted to know if she'd just imagined understanding him or actually had, she didn't have time to ask because as soon as the fairy godmother turned, the reason for his urgent barking became perfectly clear.

On the other side of the chamber, a new creature was emerging from yet another open archway. It was still another new one to Charlotte and Cat as they systematically worked their way around the chamber. It seemed that whatever laws governed the opening and closing of these portal doors preferred the pair facing something from one of the more violent, confusing worlds seen within the images. This one led into a watery setting, somewhere deep in the middle of an ocean, though Charlotte couldn't say which one or even if it belonged to Earth or EverAfter.

What she did know was that a gigantic purple-gray tentacle—a foot in diameter—was currently thrashing its way through the archway. It plummeted onto the chamber's stone floor with a wet *smack* that splashed rancid, fishy seawater in all directions.

CHAPTER TEN

"Sir Thomas? Sir Thomas, are you there? Can you hear me?"

It was Lady Charlotte's voice. Sir Thomas recognized it with as much confidence as he knew his own name and the color of his ginger coat. But he'd heard it twice, and nothing came of it. Surely, if Lady Charlotte and Cat had returned or needed him, he would know. They would show themselves or give him more effort than the occasional yell.

This wasn't an ordinary cave. It was enchanted, which meant anything could happen there. He had adventured enough to know that voice was more than likely a trick, but he couldn't shake his worry that Lady Charlotte was really calling for him.

There was an earthquake. Several, in fact. What if she's checking on us? What if she needs me?

Her voice rose through the cavern again. "Sir Thomas?"

This time, he froze and searched the darkness around him. He kept his hand on the handle of his rapier, just in case. He'd had to readjust it after all the excitement earlier, but he felt fully ready for anything now.

While he no longer clung tightly to Detective Taylor's shoulders, he kept one paw resting gently on the man's shoulder, fearing that something might cause his human charge to slip away again. Sir Thomas would once again have to chase Alex across the enormous space, the edges of which the talking cat had yet to investigate thoroughly.

He was more preoccupied with ensuring his charge's safety, but that didn't mean he wasn't suspicious of whatever lurked in the shadows. He would have preferred to check for himself, but without a guarantee that the detective wouldn't float away again, this was where he was needed most.

Charlotte's voice called him again, and he couldn't deny that there was something strange about it. At first, he thought it had been the fairy godmother. It had certainly sounded like her. Then, he had time to think before it happened again, and he wondered if he might have imagined it out of boredom and wishful thinking.

There was another option, however. Some unknown force had pulled Detective Taylor away. What if that same force had called out to Sir Thomas? What if the cave was testing him?

What if it isn't? he wondered.

No. Absolutely not. It isn't my imagination or psychosis. Cats, especially EverAfteran cats, don't go crazy. This must be something entirely different.

He waited in the semi-darkness, then let himself breathe a sigh of relief when the voice he thought he'd heard did not return.

"Phew. Well, that's one way to keep me on my toes. We'll just add it to the ever-growing list between *nearly crushed to death* and *runaway, sleep-cursed detective*. This is a mess. I hope Lady Charlotte finds what she's looking for soon." He glanced at Alex's face. The detective's eyes still moved back and forth behind closed lids. "I hope you're having a better time in your dreams than I am here. I know it sucks you're stuck like this, but at least you aren't bored."

Alex did not reply, and an interesting thought wormed its way into Sir Thomas' mind.

"This must be how you and Lady Charlotte view our conversations with Cat, hmm? I can communicate with him and understand his replies. Neither of you can hear what he says, so the bulk of it is merely educated guesses on your part. This is quite entertaining to me for some reason. Though the near constant boredom and many near-death experiences in the last, however long we've been here, might have something to do with it."

He paused. "Honestly, at this point, I think I may be questioning my sanity entirely. Not only have I been protecting *you* all day, but I've been quite nice. I even saved your life, and don't think for an instant I won't tell you *all* about it." A playful, mischievous grin curved his feline lips, and they pulled back a bit to show his tiny fangs. As fast as it came, it fell again. "Ugh. I think standing around and talking to myself all day while pretending these have been real conversations is getting to me. It's more reassuring to believe you can hear me than to think you can't."

He smiled warmly down at the motionless Detective Taylor, who still looked like he had lain down to take a quick nap, and nothing more.

Sir Thomas had only recently considered it might be better to sit and conserve his energy while waiting for Lady Charlotte and Cat to return when a voice rose again through the cavern.

"Sir Thomas? If you can hear me, please answer. I'm starting to worry about you and Alex."

Despite his hesitancy to believe it was really Charlotte speaking to him, the voice echoing across the chamber sounded so much like the fairy godmother he was having a hard time landing on a solid decision. There were too many possibilities, and any of them could have consequences. Even inaction—like not following the new path right away—had consequences.

This one posed a large risk in his opinion.

The voice grew louder and seemed to come from the other side of the cavern. Not only did it sound like the fairy godmother, but it spoke like her, too. It was the same voice, tone, and even speed. The accent was identical, and it even carried a slight wobble as Charlotte's voice did when she was worried about one of her companions.

Could it be?

"Sir Thomas!" The voice took on a scolding tone, and his chest tightened as it always did when Charlotte grew upset with him. He was always disappointed in himself for letting her down enough that she felt the need to yell at him. "There have been several earthquakes, and the cave is changing. The changes cut off my direct path back to you. I'm trying to make sure you and Alex are okay! *Please,* answer me! I trusted you to stay with him and wait for Cat and me to return. But if you've left your position, I wouldn't even know where to start looking for you in the first place."

That really *sounds like Charlotte.*

Scowling across the cavern in the direction of the voice, Sir Thomas squinted into the semi-darkness. Wherever the voice was coming from, it sounded like she was present in that very part of the cavern, like no walls were separating them.

His feline eyesight was more than sufficient to help him maneuver, but he still could not see all the way to the opposite side of the enormous underground room. Identifying Lady Charlotte's presence was impossible.

After another short period passed, when there was only silence, he let out a heavy sigh and turned his frown onto Alex. "Must simply be my wishful thinking," he murmured. "The voice sounds too close for it not to be in this room, Lady Charlotte's orb illuminates us, and you're quite literally entombed in light. If she were here, she would see us even if I couldn't see her. Maybe I *am* imagining things. It isn't like I often find myself trapped in an enchanted cave with no known exit, an unconscious human in my charge, and all while dodging falling rocks from repeated earthquakes. There isn't exactly a way to train for this. Perhaps it's starting to get to me, hmm?"

That explanation sounded perfectly reasonable to Sir Thomas, and he was content to accept it as the truth of his current mental state before a new voice echoed across the chamber, shattering the shaky confidence he had only begun to gather.

Two loud, quick, high-pitched yips echoed through the darkness, and Sir Thomas froze where he sat.

"Cat?" Sir Thomas whipped his head toward the opposite side of the chamber to scan whatever the shallow lighting would allow him to, but there was no sign of either of the two companions who had set off without him or the detective. Cat's bark sounded particularly far away, much farther than Lady Charlotte's call, but it was undoubtedly the canine within their party.

"Cat, can you hear me?" Sir Thomas shouted in excitement when he heard Cat bark again. "I'm here! Where are you?"

An unrestrained laugh echoed in response. "Oh, okay. I see how it is," Charlotte echoed. "I call for you until I'm hoarse in the throat and get no response. But if Cat barks twice, you're all about it, hmm? I see where your loyalties lie now, Sir Thomas." There was humor in her voice, just as if she'd been standing right in front of him and had said it. He could even imagine the playful smile on her face as if she was.

Sucking in a sharp breath, Sir Thomas rose to his feet and leaped forward, only to realize that his paw had left Detective Taylor's shoulder. He quickly backtracked, grabbed hold of his unconscious human charge once more, then tried again.

"Lady Charlotte," he called out, "is that really you?"

"Of course, it's really me. Who else would it be?"

He had no answer for that. Suddenly, his worry about the legitimacy of the voice and his concerns about his own sanity quickly faded.

"You've made it back?" he questioned. "Does that mean you and Cat successfully completed your portion of the quest?"

"We've finished this part, but it's far from over. Unfortunately, when the cave shifted, it cut us off. We have to find a way back to one another. Are you both all right?"

Excitement grew in Sir Thomas. "Finishing your part of the quest is fantastic news, Lady Charlotte! I did not doubt your abilities. I wish you could join us over here. I can assure you Detective Taylor is perfectly safe and unharmed, though we had a couple of close calls with falling debris in the quakes. I imagine you will want to see for yourself rather than take my word for it. Do you know where you are? Are there any noticeable landmarks around you that I can look for? "

A longer pause than he would have liked answered his question, and Sir Thomas frowned into the darkness again.

"Lady Charlotte?"

"Forgive me. I was looking around for anything I could tell you to keep an eye out for. Unfortunately, I don't see anything of use," she updated. "Also, I'm sorry about your struggles over there while alone with Alex. We've encountered a few minor obstacles of our own while we were questing."

He couldn't imagine what she and Cat had seen and experienced. He couldn't wait for all four of them to be reunited so he could hear all about it.

Sir Thomas scanned the cavern, searching for any visible damage among the falling bits of stone, rubble, dust, and debris. Despite the chaos, the majority of the cavern seemed intact. To the right, he found the soft electric blue glow of the ore tunnel where they'd initially come through. On the left, he saw that the stone archway through which Lady Charlotte and Cat had disappeared stood firm. From that distance, he couldn't tell if the archway had sustained more damage, but its shape was still discernible, which was somewhat reassuring.

"Where we are seems to be more or less unaffected, my lady," he said. "Are there any doors around you? Do you remember the direction you came from? If you found a path that led close to it, maybe you could find us. I'll stay put with the detective and wait for you and Cat to find a new way—"

"Honestly, I don't think that's an option. I'm really stumped here."

Charlotte's voice now carried a hint of concern, putting Sir Thomas on high alert. Rarely did the fairy godmother let any urgency slip into her voice, regardless of the circumstances. When she did, it usually meant something had gone horribly wrong to the point where she could no longer hide her emotions from her tone.

Sir Thomas took a step forward, guiding Alex along with him. Leaving the detective behind, even for a short distance, was unthinkable. Especially after what it had taken to reunite during the rockfall. A nagging feeling told him to stay vigilant, though he couldn't pinpoint why.

"Lady Charlotte?" he called when things had gone silent. He wasn't sure how to respond to the fairy godmother's last statement. It seemed to him that she was thinking out loud, as she often did.

"I'm still here, Sir Thomas." Her cheeriness had returned, and he wondered if she'd been trying to reel herself back in. "I think it's you who will have to come to us."

He narrowed his eyes. "I know this is probably silly, but

that concerns me. You *specifically* told me to stay put. That you'd find your way back no matter what. I'm worried moving will completely lose our path. Worst-case scenario, if you and Cat return to us, we could take Detective Taylor back through the blue tunnel and exit the way we came in. We have a guaranteed way out right now, even though it would likely take longer for the detective to recover going that route. If I continue farther into the cave with him, we might lose that exit entirely. I imagine you can understand why that would cause me to hesitate."

Another long pause followed, and then Lady Charlotte's voice returned with a semblance of concern.

"I think there's an alternate path through this cave that we might both take to meet in the middle. I can sense energy from another tunnel, but I have to find the entrance to it. I came back as far as I could, but this is as far as I can go in this direction. It's a miracle that I was able to call out to you, and you heard me."

It seemed strange she just mentioned sensing the energy from another tunnel. He wondered if that meant more of the blue ore or if she simply sensed other magic.

"How's Cat?"

"Cat is perfectly safe. He's done well and is eager to see you again. The three of us have a lot to talk about. So much has happened. Will you try? If I can find this tunnel, I'm sure it will lead us together again. I don't know if there will be any more earthquakes. I imagine we haven't seen the last of them yet. All we can do is take the paths available to us and hope they lead us back together and on to the next step."

Sir Thomas looked into the darkness that nearly encompassed the opposite side of the cavern. Everything Lady Charlotte had said sounded like her. He heard her voice with his own ears, the rise and fall of its timbre, the exact cadence of her speech. Even still, something prickled in the back of his mind that made him pause. Something still made him particularly suspicious about the current circumstances.

"Sir Thomas?" Charlotte called again. "Is everything all right? Are you able to move? Can you still hear me?"

"I'm still here, my lady," he replied. "We're safe and sound. Sorry about that. I'm looking around the cavern and thinking about this. I'm still not entirely certain I'm okay with leaving our current position to join you. This whole scenario seems rather—"

He was interrupted by two of Cat's sharp barks in quick succession. It seemed like a reasonable response on Cat's part to urge his fellow furry friend into action. The difficulty, however, was that Sir Thomas could not make out any words within the barks, merely the urgency of them rising in response to his hesitation.

Then again, this could have been important enough that Cat didn't offer any words with his interruption. Maybe he was just trying to capture Sir Thomas' attention to get him moving again.

"I don't think we have much time," Charlotte called, her voice echoing across the cavern. "Another earthquake could happen at any moment, and if it does, it could cut us off even more so than we are right now. I know I told you to stay put and wait for us, but plans have changed. When on a journey or a quest, that happens. It's why you have to stay quick on your feet. I don't know what else to do. Please help me, Sir Thomas."

Guilt flooded him as he considered her words. He'd never made her beg him for his help before, and it made him feel terrible. "Of course, my lady. Just a moment."

He needed to think. He needed time. Though her pleas sounded genuine, like the very godmother he knew, and Cat's bark was unmistakable, something still felt off about the situation. Sir Thomas sensed it keenly but couldn't justify or explain his hesitation. When he considered the flow of her words, how she spoke to them, and everything she'd said, it all fit.

So, why can't I trust her?

What has gotten into me?

We're supposed to be together as one party for this quest. That's the vow I made. So, what is keeping me?

The question was easier asked than answered, and no immediate explanations for his hesitation came to mind. The talking cat turned toward his unconscious human charge and raised an eyebrow. "Would you be surprised to learn, Detective, that now is one of those rare moments during which I would be particularly grateful for your opinion? It would make it so much easier if you could discuss this with me."

After narrowing his eyes at the apparent source of the voices on the opposite side of the cavern, Sir Thomas took a step back to stand closer to the unconscious floating form in his care and kept his mouth shut.

He couldn't shake it, but something told him to stay put. *I really hope this isn't a mistake.*

He wondered if this was the best way to respond: with

silence. He hadn't taken a course of action before, and the cave *told* him what to do. What if no direct course of action was needed now? If he were *supposed* to find the fairy godmother, surely the cave would push the matter.

Sometimes, Lady Charlotte's earlier advice was particularly suited to a situation.

Just wait and see–

And that was precisely what Sir Thomas intended to do. He found himself unable to focus on anything else as he waited for confirmation of his concerns or some sign that he was being overly cautious and had unnecessarily taken up more of the party's time.

He felt remarkably vindicated when no further calls for him to join them rose from the darkness beyond. It supported his suspicions that this was not real but a trick of his mind or the result of something magical within the enchanted cave.

Sir Thomas was sure the new stone archway with light coming through it was not a hallucination. He had slapped a paw against its perimeter several times to assure himself he was not imagining things. It truly was a new path.

However, as promised, he had no intention of leaving the cavern until Lady Charlotte and Cat returned. He almost believed they had, but without visual proof, there was no telling who or what actually waited for him where the voices had originated.

It was not a risk he was willing to take.

CHAPTER ELEVEN

A thick tentacle squirmed out of the portal before smashing against the wall to the right. Within seconds, another slithered through before smacking against the wall to the left.

Charlotte and Cat both backed up, each of them staring helplessly in horror as they watched the monster use its suctioned grip on the stone walls to pull itself through. Since coming to Cincinnati, Alex had introduced her to the internet and things like YouTube. She'd seen videos of octopi squishing themselves into whatever shape was needed to escape through tiny exits.

Their bodies were gelatinous and capable of collapsing as they slowly pulled themselves through impossibly small holes to achieve their goal, and she was seeing it happen in real-time now.

The massive beast made wet, squelching noises as it squeezed through the archway. The scent of saltwater and rot filled the room, nearly causing Charlotte's stomach to roll. As more tentacles freed themselves, water poured into the room, quickly submerging the floor in an inch or two of seawater.

One of the slithering appendages arched across the room and slapped down only five feet away from Charlotte, spraying smelly water all over her and Cat. The floor trembled so badly that Charlotte's knees buckled, and she dropped to her hands and knees. Her dress and cloak were soaked, and when she lifted her hands, a layer of slime dripped off.

I'm going to be sick, she thought.

Cat barked, and words flowed through her head as if she'd heard a different language and immediately translated it. *Fight it before it fully comes through, before it's at full strength.*

What she now knew was Cat's inner voice speaking in her head finally pulled her out of her dazed state. Her head jerked in his direction, and he barked again before growling.

"Good plan."

She climbed to her feet and leaped back, narrowly dodging the tentacle that had landed right next to her moments before. She wiped her hands off on the driest part of her dress to make sure that the hold on her wand was tight.

Red light glowed from the tip of the wand before another barrier appeared around them. "Get ready, Cat. I don't know how well this barrier will hold up against something that big and strong. The second I strike, those tentacles are going to thrash."

I'm ready, he yipped.

She shook her head. "That'll take some getting used to."

Facing the threat slowly squeezing its way through the tiny archway, she took a deep breath. "Let's see if I can deep fry it."

With only the flick of her wand, she chased the water out of the barrier, leaving only the circle inside of it where they stood completely dry. It would need to be for her to do what came next. The wand glowed even brighter, the light turning a vibrant blue before she flung her arm forward.

A lightning bolt shot forward, connecting with the soft underbelly just as it started to squeeze through the portal. Lightning webbed out from the spot of impact, striking the walls and wet floor, no doubt sending an electric charge through the water as she'd expected. Despite there not being a mouth that she could see in the portion of the body that had made it through, a dark, *loud*, guttural roar shook the cavern chamber.

Hit it again! Cat barked, his paws tapping excitedly on the stone.

Charlotte was just about to raise her wand when the tentacle that had landed close to her hit the side of the barrier *hard*. The barrier acted like a bubble around them, moving with them as the Kraken punted them across the chamber.

The magic inside the shield acted like pillows, softening the blow as well as their landing, but they still hit the floor hard.

"*Ugh*," Charlotte grunted. "I guess that's what happens when something hits the barrier."

The falling debris from earlier created a downward force, so the barrier had no reason to move. A sideswipe appeared to be much different. She wondered if she could somehow root it to the ground so they wouldn't go flying again if struck.

Each of the four tentacles that were in the chamber thrashed from side to side, searching for its attacker to do more damage. The one closest to them was the problem, and she got an idea.

"Cat, you're getting the Alex treatment."

The Newfoundland looked up at her only a moment before silvery light encased him and lifted him off the ground.

"If I fly, the barrier will follow me, but you won't. Now, you'll float with me, and the barrier will close around us entirely. I'll fight it from the air. The tentacles are attacking at ground level."

Cat didn't have time to respond because another tentacle swung at them. Charlotte beat her wings as quickly as she could, lifting off and getting them to safety, but narrowly missing the attack by inches.

She flew to the center of the room and didn't hesitate to charge her magic again. The wand turned bright blue, and she aimed. Another lightning bolt bigger than the last hit the beast in what she now saw was an eye as a giant lid opened only a heartbeat before she struck it with lightning.

It landed with a loud *pop!* and webbed out again as dark purple goop oozed out of the eye. A beak came through the archway and opened to scream in pain in the room. Cat howled in pain, and Charlotte's eyes closed as she covered her ears instinctively. She could already hear the ringing, and she imagined her companion felt much worse.

Charlotte! Cat's sharp bark brought her back to the present.

She turned just in time to see two of the tentacles swipe at her from each side, the suction cups landing on the barrier with a loud sucking sound. She peered through the small gap between them to see the injured eye open again and fixed right on her.

"How the hell can it see after that?!"

Lightning isn't working, Cat whined.

The tentacles encircled them, and she started to panic. *What-do-I-do, what-do-I-do?*

Another tentacle slithered out of the door, and along with it came more of the body. It didn't seem to have any kind of armor. She could see the apparent damage she'd caused, so the lightning *had* injured it, but it wasn't enough. It was too big, too powerful.

The barrier around them held firm as the tentacles squeezed. She could feel the pressure through the energy of her magic, but they were safe—for now.

That wouldn't necessarily stay the case though, so she knew she needed to act fast. *The barrier... It's solid to the monster.*

Charlotte could manipulate the shape of the barrier if the need ever arose. However, that had never happened until now.

With a slight flick of her wrist, a spike speared through one of the suction cups, and once again, a howl filled the air as the beast screamed in pain. At that moment, Charlotte realized its body was just as squishy and vulnerable as any other squid or octopus.

Lifting both of her hands, she rotated them, causing the

barrier to spin. The slimy tentacles simply slid over it since they couldn't grip the magic as it moved. As the barrier spun, creating a bit of a wind tunnel inside, blowing around her hair and Cat's fur, Charlotte opened her hand.

Spikes jutted forward, grating the tentacles that held them and spraying dark purple blood all over the barrier and down to the floor below. The tentacles jerked back, and water splashed into the air as the beast thrashed around in pain below.

Charlotte didn't have any projectiles, and straight magical energy wasn't working. She needed a weapon—something to spear it and kill it. Unlike the confused wyrmling, *this* thing she had no qualms about killing.

The injured tentacles splashed down, and water arced through the air, giving her an idea. The tip of her wand turned a turquoise blue as she gained control of the water below them. She watched carefully as the body fully emerged. Now that it was out and the rest of the tentacles would soon follow, she needed to get this just right, or they wouldn't stand a chance.

The monster rose to its full height, its large, bulbous head turned directly toward her. The other eye opened, and she knew this was her chance. It had no armor, and its body was fully visible now.

"I know what I need to do," she said.

At first, she'd thought to freeze the monster to buy her time. But another idea suddenly came to mind.

Charlotte began to move her wand, causing the water below to twist and churn. The monster's attention pulled away, and the moment it was distracted, she took her chance.

Swinging like a coach just called her up to bat in one of those games Alex enjoyed watching in his free time, she let loose a wave of magical energy. The water below shot forward, freezing into thousands of icy spikes before tearing through the body of the beast.

Wet, gurgling screams tore through the air as its tentacles twitched, thrashed, and then slowed. Time seemed to stand still as the room went quiet. The creature wobbled for several long seconds as its tentacles slipped away from the wall to slowly fall before splashing into the water below.

Finally, after what felt like forever, the bulbous head collapsed, and the entire creature went limp.

Exhausted, Charlotte focused on what energy it took to fly and nothing else. She needed to get rid of the water and the body somehow before she would land in the bloody sea water below.

"It took that thing *forever* to come through the portal," Charlotte panted. "Do you think I can just...*shove* it back through?"

Before Cat had a chance to answer, loud cracks and pops echoed around the room as the walls started to spin. Just as before, the sound grew overwhelming, but it seemed it wasn't quite as bad with them in the air.

"What the hell?" she breathed. "Again?"

The Kraken's two tentacles that remained within the portal were instantly severed as the room spun and tossed the beast to the side. The movement created what appeared to be a vacuum effect. The water was pulled from the center of the chamber to pool around the stone walls. The portal began to suck the rancid seawater back into its realm.

The monster's limp limbs rolled and moved with the force, but the body seemed too heavy. The tips of three of the tentacles pulled through the archway along with the water. Once the room was clear, the spinning ground to a halt, and the portal closed, effectively severing the tentacles at the threshold.

"Oh, *come on!*" Charlotte complained. "You're just going to leave us here with that smelly beast? It stank *before!* It's going to rot and smell ten times worse now!" She sighed and turned to Cat. "Well, this should be fun."

The fairy godmother lowered them to the cavern floor now that it was clear of most of the evidence from their battle. Aside from the mutilated Kraken corpse—which was now smashed against the wall from the force of the room spinning before—there was no evidence anything had happened in there.

She sat, and Cat immediately flopped down beside her. "Are your ears okay?" she asked. She had a mild headache from all the noise, but it wasn't nearly as bad as before.

Cat gave a low whine, and somehow, she understood that it was his way of saying he was fine. It still baffled her how she randomly gained the ability to hear him, but she wasn't about to look a gift horse in the mouth. Or a gift dog, in this case. She'd take any advantage she could get.

She laid back. "I need no less than three scalding hot showers, then to sleep for about a week, a pound of choco-late, a gallon of wine, and a binge fest of my favorite shows." She was exhausted, and that sounded perfect to her. "Not necessarily in that order. Minus the shower. Pretty sure I'm still covered in suction cup goop. *Bleh.*"

Magical energy bloomed, and Charlotte's head darted up so she could inspect the direction it came from. Another one of the archways glowed as it seemingly *switched on.* She couldn't make out the landscape inside, but she clearly saw what looked like a giant bear walking around inside.

Dread filled her as she stilled, waiting for what would happen next. When nothing came out, her eyes narrowed. "I think it's letting us know another challenge is coming, but we have time before it does."

Cat laid his head on her stomach as he snuggled in closer, and he whined again. *Rest.*

She snorted and relaxed back. "You don't have to tell me twice. I have a feeling I'm going to need it. Will you know if something is about to come out? If I fall asleep, will we be safe?"

The Newfoundland whined. *Sleep. I'll know before anything approaches the portal.*

A heavy sigh of relief flooded through her, and she relaxed on the cavern floor. Oddly enough, it became more and more comfortable every time she did. She imagined that had more to do with her exhaustion than her actually liking it.

"Cat, I'm so glad I brought you with me. I don't know what I'd do without you."

CHAPTER TWELVE

The silence around Sir Thomas stretched for several long minutes until he started to grow more comfortable with his circumstances. The more time that passed, the more likely it seemed that he had imagined the voices.

He started to believe that being stuck here alone with the unconscious detective, with nothing else to occupy his mind, had led him to this state. His mind had devised a way to entertain itself. The more he thought about it, the likelier that scenario seemed, and his comfort and confidence returned.

That was, until the next earthquake ripped through the cavern.

It couldn't have been longer than ten minutes since he'd last heard Charlotte's voice when a new tremor raced through the enormous underground space. Just as Sir Thomas had feared, the cavern around him and Detective Taylor was forcing his hand. He realized there no choice now. Sir Thomas needed to move them to safety, or the falling debris would crush him and Alex both. This tremor seemed intent on tearing the chamber apart entirely, forcing the talking cat to consider options he previously wouldn't have.

Within the first few seconds of the earthquake, an enormous slab of rock began to crack and split away from the stone wall where Sir Thomas had sought refuge with the detective. He heard the stone wall protesting under the effects of the earthquake and looked up in time to see the slab break away before hurtling down toward them. The slab crashed against the cavern wall as it fell, breaking into several smaller chunks, all still large enough to cause severe damage if they did not get out of there immediately.

Sir Thomas' first thought was to head for the stone archway Charlotte and Cat had taken when they'd left the chamber. However, he quickly scrapped that idea when he remembered that the fairy godmother had already tried to bring Alex through that same archway, and the cave had barred her from passing with the detective in tow.

Sir Thomas slapped both paws down on Alex's shoulders and hurried out of the way of the rock threatening to crush them while pushing the detective ahead of him. The fairy godmother's magic made it easy to maneuver Alex, as if the human weighed nothing at all. Otherwise, Sir Thomas would have had a hard time getting them to safety.

The choice now was to move to a safer part of the large cavern room they were in or go through the new door leading to the unknown tunnel he'd been hesitant to explore. Deep down, Sir Thomas knew the quest cave was trying to urge him on, but it worried him since he was alone with a charge.

If I stay, there will only be more quakes until I'm exhausted of all options and forced through the door.

A different wall seemed largely unaffected, and Sir Thomas pushed himself faster in that direction, knowing they would be much safer there until he could think and come to an educated decision rather than one made in a panic. At least there was less chance of being crushed by falling debris in the spot he'd found.

For now.

Rock, earth, and clouds of dirt rained down around the swashbuckling cat as he struggled to direct his precious cargo. The detective may have been light, but he was still large and difficult to steer.

Sir Thomas yowled when a larger stone clipped his shoulder. Unable to stop and check on the wound, he let out a hiss of frustration and pain before continuing to steer Alex left and then right. He managed to avoid the worst of the falling chunks, but he had no idea how long he could keep it up.

Then, a familiar voice called to him from the other side of the cavern, barely audible above the din of booming, breaking boulders and stone shards.

"Sir Thomas! You have to head to the new tunnel! You'll both be safer there!"

Once again, it was Lady Charlotte's voice. Sir Thomas thought he could hear his good friend Cat barking in the distance, too. His immediate reaction was to reject the proposal, mainly because he still didn't trust the owner of that voice. After all, if it was really her, how would she have known where safety was if she was, in fact, separated from him? He didn't believe it was the real Charlotte Weaver, and if it was, something was very wrong with her.

Maybe it isn't Charlotte... But what if the enchanted cave is urging me on to the next important step by using her voice since it knows I trust her?

He'd assumed the whole time that if the owner of the voice wasn't the fairy godmother, it was something or someone malevolent. Now, he wondered if the cave was trying to help him along.

Regardless, time had run out, and he had no other options. The first stone archway was gone, the cavern was on the verge of collapsing, and he refused to endanger his own life or Detective Taylor's. It no longer mattered to him that Lady Charlotte had asked him to take on that duty. It only mattered that Alex was part of their team, and he wouldn't leave him behind.

"This way! You can make it!"

At the sound of the lady Charlotte's voice urging him onward, Sir Thomas spun with Alex sticking straight out in front of him and forced himself into an urgent speed he rarely had cause to call upon. Right now, however, was one of those instances when anything less than every ounce of power he had wouldn't do.

The bobbing orb of glowing light Charlotte had left with them raced after him no matter which direction he moved. More than light, the orb caused confusion and frustration as its wild bobbing and swaying cast moving shadows across the floor and walls, interfering with Sir Thomas' ability to detect the falling boulders around him as quickly as he would have liked.

But then he found another light, the soft glow coming

from the edge of the cavern in front of him and the second stone archway which had only appeared once the earthquakes began.

He ran hard with everything he had. Soon, there would be nothing else left, and he hoped all his efforts would be enough. He likely wouldn't have another chance otherwise.

Another enormous slab of stone, like the first that had blocked the other archway, sliced away from the cavern and plummeted straight toward him.

With another yowl of effort and silently praying to whatever magical entity might be listening, Sir Thomas threw himself forward, pushing Alex along in front of him. He saw the shadow of the falling slab of rock darkening over his extended arms and paws and the top of Alex's head in front of him. He fought the urge to clench his eyes shut in fear.

A loud breath whooshed out of him as he skidded across the cold stone as he rushed through the archway. He hit the floor hard before tumbling over several times and finally landing with his back against the far wall. His eyes opened the moment the chunk of stone crashed just on the other side of the archway with a jolting tremor followed by a gust of cool, dank wind and a roiling dust cloud that burst through the now-blocked archway. The sound deafened him and filled his sensitive ears with a painful ringing.

Pain split through Sir Thomas' head, and he reached up to take off his hat. His paw rubbed the back just behind his ears, and he hissed in pain. He realized he must have hit it when he'd flattened against the wall.

More crashing rumbles and ominous cracks reverberated from within the cavern. Specks of minerals shimmered in the low light, peppering his orange coat and irritating his nose and eyes.

When it finally was over, Sir Thomas took a moment to collect himself, breathing heavily and listening for any other signs of imminent danger. Hearing none, he blinked out the last of the dust and mineral particles from his eyes, shook himself head to toe to clear the rubble from his fur, put his hat back on, and looked around the darkness of his new surroundings.

There was still some light, though it was muted and sparse. Sir Thomas realized that Charlotte's conjured orb of light had been trapped behind the slab of stone now blocking the archway. He noted two sources of shallow light within his reach.

The first and brightest came from the magic surrounding Detective Taylor, who floated a mere yard away. From the looks of things, his rough entrance must not have damaged him in any way like it had Sir Thomas. As annoyed as the cat was at having a splitting headache, ringing ears, and a sore shoulder, he was grateful that Charlotte's protective magic had indeed sheltered Alex from the worst of the backlash and debris.

The silvery white glow of the protective magic lit up enough of the corridor for Sir Thomas to assess their situation. Coming closer, the feisty cat saw that Alex really did seem perfectly fine. No dirt or debris covered his prone body, and there were no dark spots or patches of blood. The detective looked healthy and in mint condition, which was exactly what Sir Thomas had hoped to see.

When his heart finally stopped pounding, Sir Thomas

tried to settle his nerves. His filthy coat bothered him immensely, but it was a problem he'd have to solve later. Right now, the detective's safety was of the utmost importance, and Sir Thomas did not intend to let himself get distracted any more than either of them could afford.

He circled Detective Taylor, pausing every few steps to scan the new corridor for any lurking threats or potential aftershocks from the frequent earthquakes. As far as he could tell, nothing else threatened them here, so he made it back to Alex's side to thoroughly inspect his charge.

Saving them both from the imminent destruction of the cavern was one thing, but failing in his duty to preserve the detective's well-being was another matter entirely. After a quick but thorough inspection of Alex's prone form, Sir Thomas sighed in relief and leaned against the wall.

"We've made it, Detective. After all that, we made it. Honestly, I wasn't entirely sure this would be the outcome when that last slab fell away, but fortunately for both of us, you are conveniently light. It made it possible for me to get us out of there in one piece."

Placing a paw firmly on the detective's shoulder, Sir Thomas let the solid warmth of Alex's presence reassure him. He returned to studying their surroundings and noticed a second, dimmer source of light coming from around the corner where the narrow corridor continued.

"There we are, Detective. It seems the rest of this passage may yet hold something in store for us, and I intend to keep my word to both you and Lady Charlotte. I plan to ensure your safety and fulfill my vow to Lady Charlotte by waiting for her and Cat to return. I don't know if that voice I keep hearing is her or not, and after it urged us to safety, I worry I might have misjudged the situation. It might truly be her. So, you and I will be spending the rest of this quest here in this tunnel instead of exploring the wide-open, dark spaces of the chamber. Besides, after everything that just happened, we've lost our only source of light."

Sir Thomas pulled Alex's motionless, near-weightless form with him farther down the tunnel until he reached the bend. On the other side, a second source of light flowed toward them. The talking cat wanted to settle the detective in an area with more light to help him better watch his charge and help him feel safer.

He had no intention of continuing around the bend or exploring further, especially not with Detective Taylor in tow. He had promised Lady Charlotte that they would wait. Being forced out of the cavern by impending death surely counted as an extenuating circumstance, and he was confident Lady Charlotte would understand the predicament without being too upset with him for the change in plans. He hoped.

Instead, he chose to settle for waiting within this new tunnel, safe behind the now entirely blocked archway. He was content to rest here.

Unfortunately, the cavern had other plans.

As soon as Sir Thomas felt himself getting quite comfortable on the floor, with his back resting against the stone wall and Alex hovering in the air beside him within arm's reach, the voice he now questioned disturbed his rest again.

"Sir Thomas, please tell me you made it out of there safely. I can't quite tell…"

He started at the sound of her voice. Hope once again filled him that this was really Lady Charlotte, the fairy godmother and leader of their group. As he'd told Alex, the fact that she had urged him toward the safety of this corridor at the last moment—when it seemed all other options were out of the question—had returned some of his confidence and belief the voice really did belong to Lady Charlotte.

Nothing that means us any harm would have done such a thing to save us from the entire cavern falling in upon our heads. This must be her.

He cleared his throat and lifted his chin to reply. "We're here, my lady! Detective Taylor and I made it safely through, thanks to your timely instruction. We'll wait here for you and Cat to find your way through the labyrinth so we can continue our journey together."

"If only we could." There was a slight discomfort in the fairy godmother's voice, but it quickly disappeared when she added, "We have to look for each other, Sir Thomas. Is the tunnel you're in still open enough for you to continue, or was it narrowed in the recent quake?"

Sir Thomas leaned against the wall to peer around the corner where a softer light emanated. Then he called out, "I believe it's wide enough to get through, my lady."

"Then continue through the tunnel, Sir Thomas. Another archway opened for us, so we now have a path to start on as well. We'll find each other; I know we will. No matter what, make sure you bring the human with you. If the path is too narrow, try to find another way. We can't leave him behind."

"As you wish, my lady."

With a heavy sigh, Sir Thomas stood, dusted himself off again, and turned toward Alex's floating form shrouded in the fairy godmother's magic. "If you heard that, Detective, you and I are about to go on our own little journey so that we can find Lady Charlotte and Cat. It shouldn't take long. I have a feeling the bulk of the danger is now behind us."

He sighed. "Even if you were still completely immobile, I wish you were at least alert. That way, if you noticed any other impending dangers, you could tell me. Regardless, we shall continue as we have. I have every faith that you will do whatever you can the moment you are able. Soon, we'll be within the warm, reassuring company of the other half of our party."

He took hold of Alex's shoulders and proceeded to push the feather-light detective around the corner of the dimly lit tunnel, deeper into the quest cave as Lady Charlotte had instructed.

Because Sir Thomas had grown so used to talking down to Alex and referring to him as "the human," it didn't even occur to him until just now to think it was strange that Charlotte had referred to him that way.

But as soon as he thought it, he brushed it off.

After all, if something terrible was after them, why would it have saved them?

CHAPTER THIRTEEN

Charlotte was exhausted, and Cat wasn't faring much better. She'd lost count of all the battles they'd fought. At this point, she had no idea how long they'd been in there. It always seemed that once a challenge ended, a couple of hours would pass before the next one came along.

The enchanted cave had given her hell, but it also let her rest between each match.

But once again, the fight was on, and she was already wearing down. Even when an opponent looked relatively non-threatening, like a group of crows, they turned out to be *far* more challenging than she'd assessed them to be.

A violent plume of flame spewed down toward Charlotte's head. Ducking swiftly, she managed to release a spray of deep blue light, which formed into a gushing stream of water aimed directly at her adversary.

A furious squawk confirmed her spell had hit its mark, but she didn't have time to search for the three-eyed crow among the many others she and Cat were battling. More of them were now bearing down on the fairy godmother and her furry companion, and avoiding being burned to a crisp took priority over watching one succumb to her watery attack.

"Cat, behind you!"

He'd already recognized the danger and spun around to face it before Charlotte finished her warning. With a snarl, he lurched to the side, dodging another burst of deep orange flame from the open beak of one three-eyed crow, then another. When the coast was clear, Cat launched himself off the ground toward his prey. His incredible agility was no surprise to Charlotte, especially since the enchanted dog had once been a cat, but the height of his leap was astounding.

His large, powerful jaws clamped down around the body of one of the offending crows, which let out a horrid, pain-filled squawk before Cat crushed the life out of it between his jaws. He landed gracefully on all fours, shook his head instinctively to assure himself of the crow's demise, and spat the three-eyed corpse onto the floor of the circular chamber.

Plumes of purple feathers, so dark they were almost black, spewed from his jaws. One hung from his tongue as he panted while looking over to check on the fairy godmother.

Charlotte managed to take down two more beastly creatures careening toward her companion with a single blast of blinding golden light, which captured the crows in a web of magic.

The fairy godmother jerked roughly on her wand, tightening the magical web until she smashed both three-eyed crows together. They crashed to the ground in a tangle of sharp talons, beaks, and trapped wings. The two lashed out, effectively ripping one another to shreds and making Charlotte's job easier.

More purple-black feathers sprayed into the air, coating the chamber floor with the plumage of both party members' latest foes. The feathers piled up, gleaming in the low light of the fairy godmother's conjured orbs like enormous puddles of spilled oil gathering on the stone beneath them. Dozens of three-eyed crow bodies littered the chamber, and still, it seemed the murderous onslaught would never end.

Cat fought admirably, leaping to unexpected heights and executing astonishing acrobatic feats midair to bring down the endless onslaught of crows swarming around them. In one leap, he caught two birds in his jaws, pinning them together by their wings before landing and setting upon them with all the strength and fury his size afforded him.

Charlotte caught five more crows within her magical net of shimmering light, pulling the strings tight as she swung her wand left and right. Deciding quickness and efficiency were required, she gave a forceful downward swing, smashing the trapped birds against the stone floor before moving on to repeat the process.

The various colors in the flickers of magic from each successive spell zipped across the chamber, lighting up the archways still filled with shimmering scenes from different worlds and realms.

When it seemed they would have to fight these crows for an eternity, the final trio of birds hurtled through the most recently opened archway, headed straight for the fairy godmother. She got one of them with a quickly thrown spell but wasn't fast enough to capture the last two.

The first crow to reach her dove at her neck, clipping her with its sharp beak. The fairy godmother cried out in pain as she spun away from her winged adversary. The movement conveniently took her out of the way of a growling Cat as he leaped through the air to catch the crow that had clipped her.

His jaws clamped around the bird, and he crushed it as he spun around and leaped toward the third and final three-eyed crow. His unwavering grace would have been a treat to watch had Charlotte not been fighting for her life at the same time.

The giant dog leaped for the third crow just as it dove for an attack. Cat's enormous front paws pummeled the bird, pinning it beneath his weight before touching down on the stone floor. The sound of his claws clacking against the floor joined the sickening crunch of the crow's body breaking beneath his paws.

Without paying further attention to the creature beneath him, Cat snarled and growled through a mouthful of feathers as the bird struggled uselessly in his jaws. He'd already crushed the beast, but it had yet to die. It let out a few dying squawks, the last of which cut off abruptly with a strangled croak when Cat shook his head vigorously. His powerful jaws and neck whipped the bird far more than its body could handle.

Charlotte heard the awful snapping and crackling of the final crow's bones breaking beneath Cat's deadly grip but didn't waste any more time watching. Instead, she scanned the chamber for any wayward crows that might have slipped past the fairy godmother and her loyal companion.

Breathing heavily, Charlotte held her wand at the ready, sweat coating her forehead and dripping down her cheeks. She swiped it away from her eyes with the back of her hand, then absently reached up to relieve the tickling itch trailing down her neck. Warm, sticky wetness came away on her hand, and she glanced down to see her blood smeared across her knuckles.

Even the sting from the three-eyed crow's beak didn't fully capture her attention. This was a battle—an incredibly dangerous, magical, and seemingly endless battle she and Cat had been fighting for longer than she could justify.

Their latest opponent had surged through the most recent archway, a flock of dozens of three-eyed crows. Initially, they didn't seem like much of a threat until dark orange flames began to spray from their open beaks.

Now, after several moments of panting in the center of the chamber—wand at the ready, sweat and blood trickling across her skin, and her heart pounding in her ears—she realized they had once again reached a brief reprieve from their struggles. They were trapped in this circular chamber, which had sealed all exits, forcing the fairy godmother and her canine companion to face foe after foe.

And they kept coming.

Finally assured that his prey was really dead, Cat opened his mouth and released the carcass of the final three-eyed crow. The tiny body fell to the chamber's stone floor, rolling once in a tangle of shredded plumage and damp bloodstains before coming to rest in a lump that would have been unidentifiable if they didn't already know what it was.

Cat removed his paws from atop the other crow, sniffed the lifeless husk, then licked his chops and looked eagerly up at the fairy godmother. His tongue was stained a deep crimson. It flopped from his mouth as he panted, his tail swinging side-to-side before the exhaustion of their recent battle caught up to him.

Once he realized the same thing that the fairy godmother had, that their battle had reached its end, his tail drooped in fatigue. Still, he didn't look away from Charlotte, and the question in his eyes was perfectly clear to her.

Taking a deep breath, she closed her eyes and smoothed the damp, sticky hair away from her face before letting out a massive sigh. "I'm fine, Cat. Thanks for asking. However, I would feel *much* better if we could steal enough time away from uselessly battling creatures from all over multiple universes to find ourselves a way out of this place. I'm starting to think we took a drastically wrong turn somewhere within the tunnel that led us here. Perhaps my eagerness to continue on this quest of ours got the better of me, and I missed the path we should have taken. I can't imagine this is where we're supposed to be...that this is where Fate intended to lead us."

She had lost all sense of time in this circular chamber. The glowing archways once contained an unidentified, opalescent substance Charlotte and Cat had discovered during their trek through the tunnel that led them here. Now, each archway held a scene from a different world, kingdom, realm, planet, or maybe even universe.

It wouldn't have surprised the fairy godmother if those doorways also led to different points in time. But she understood there would be no testing that theory for her and her furry companion.

This chamber was not a hall of doorways for adventurers to explore other realms. Instead, it was a battle arena where adventurers came to kill or be killed, facing one monstrous creature after another coming through the open portals. The beasts wasted no time discovering who the adventurers were or why they had arrived. Their only intention was to surge inside, agitated either by the breach into their world or by the presence of a fairy godmother and a large, furry black dog on their personal quest.

They could have been there for hours, or they could have been there days—weeks, even. The laws of magic and quests she'd learned in the Guild and in her own experiences had ceased to follow the constructs she believed would always govern them.

The first sign was the chamber eliminating all possible exit routes. When the tunnel that led them here ceased to exist, Charlotte knew this would be a far greater challenge than she'd anticipated. Trying to discern how each of the shimmering doorways worked had been a hard lesson in patience and thinking outside the box.

Charlotte's attempts to stick her hand through one of the archways, only for her fingers to get covered in the pearly goop before she flicked the remnants off onto the floor, causing their present hell to begin, weren't exactly in any of the scattered pages of her handbook.

Every detail about their time in this chamber was new to the fairy godmother; her previous knowledge was rendered useless when nothing reacted, responded, or existed the way it was supposed to.

Then came the creatures.

The wyrmling that Charlotte had first assumed to be nothing more than part of a moving picture within the archway remained the only creature she and Cat had fought that had escaped with its life. If Charlotte had known she and her companion would be stuck here, forced to battle creature after creature from hidden lands, she might not have used such a powerful spell to send the wyrmling back through the archway. She would have saved her power and killed it.

Then again, there was no telling what else she could have done if she had known anything about this place. She'd nearly used the extent of her power to send the wyrmling back home and away from eating either her or Cat. Despite that, Charlotte and Cat had successfully battled every other menacing critter, beast, and monster these shimmering doorways had sent their way.

In the current silence filling the chamber, Charlotte took a moment to assess their status. On the opposite side of the chamber lay the carcass of the enormous sea Kraken they took down after the wyrmling's escape. Nearby were the bodies of two large bears, each boasting long spiked tails that seemed more fitting for a dragon or an ancient lizard from some desert wasteland.

After the bears had come the chimera, which Charlotte had loathed to battle. No matter how hard she tried to reason with the creature, its three heads would not give in, and it fought her and Cat to the bitter end.

Everywhere the fairy godmother looked, carcasses of

defeated animals lay strewn about. By her count, she and Cat had now faced twelve battles against beasts emerging from each newly opened archway along the chamber's circular walls. The murder of three-eyed crows had made it thirteen.

The doorways didn't seem to open in any pattern. The only warning was a trembling bellow, deafening screech, or snarling growl before something lumbered out of its world into the hidden chamber.

Charlotte wasn't so sure anymore that they had entered a *true* quest cave, one blessed by the Fate that governed magic, adventure, and legendary stories. This was all wrong and defied every rule she knew. It was battle and death without reason. The foes varied in strength.

The wyrmling, which had been the first, was among one of the strongest. Though, she might not have had such a terrible time if her goal had been to kill it versus preserving its life and sending it back home. The Kraken was much stronger and threatening, but the bears weren't nearly the task the previous two had been.

The rules for things like this started easy and grew harder. Each level or challenge increased in difficulty to measure the hero's resolve, their strength, and their determination to save the day. Nothing was going well. It was like some wide-eyed novice was running the show.

She just imagined them sitting around somewhere, calling all the shots. Just grabbing whatever they found handy to shove through the portals for her to fight. It made *no* sense. It was annoying at first, mostly because she didn't understand. But the longer it went on, the more confident she became that this was something else entirely.

That just flat-out ticked her off.

Still, Charlotte's only option was to continue with Cat by her side, preparing for each new doorway to open and reveal another creature, whether familiar from her training or entirely unknown.

It seemed they might never get out of there if things continued this way, but fortunately, both Charlotte and Cat were incredibly stubborn. Neither of them was willing to give up. They would continue until they made it through to whatever the other side held for them or until one of these creatures gained the upper hand and did them in first.

She looked across the chamber and found Cat again. He was busy licking his paw, which was either his way of preparing for another fight or caring for a wound Charlotte couldn't see.

"How are you doing over there, Cat?" she asked, raising her eyebrows and nodding in his direction.

He stopped licking his paw and let out a single high-pitched yip, trap continuing to stare at her.

"You're not telling me anything I don't know, friend," the fairy godmother replied, gesturing to the creature carnage around them. "This was not what I expected either. Nor do I find anything about this chamber honorable or exciting. If I knew how to get us out of here, I would. Trust me. I'm no longer interested in finishing whatever this is. There's nothing here. It's a trap. I just can't figure out who trapped us here."

He cocked his head at her, looking more contemplative than confused. *What comes next? Are you okay? You're bleeding.*

Charlotte shook her head. "I have no idea what comes next, but yes. I'm doing fine, thank you. A bit of a nick on the neck." Charlotte reached toward the wound where the three-eyed crow's beak had sliced through her skin. She felt the sticky, slightly dried blood flaking away beneath her fingers. "At least it's small enough to heal quickly."

She turned her attention to the carcasses littering the chamber floor and shook her head. "This is awful. I know these poor creatures. I would have loved to help them back through those archways into their own world again, but clearly, that wasn't an option. They're beautiful birds. Three eyes like that... Did you know that is a tried-and-true marker of possessing The Sight? I wonder what else they might have been responsible for in their world. Instead, they're here, responsible only for keeping you and me busy while we struggle to figure out who the hell lured and trapped us here in the first place. And without a doubt, I now believe that's the case."

Before the fairy godmother could say anything else, the growling, roaring rumble she and her furry companion had come to know so well filled the chamber once again, and her relaxed posture disappeared.

"Not again..." She looked at Cat with wide eyes, her stomach sinking at the prospect of another battle so soon. "This can't be right. It's too soon! We've been given time to rest all this time. I think we should—"

The violent rumbling of the walls spinning around them cut her off, but that hardly mattered anymore. Cat was already on his way to her, leaping over the bodies of different creatures that were littering the chamber floor. He reached the fairy godmother's side and flopped down, sticking his head between her calves. She pinned his ears with her legs while she covered her own. Their new ritual after so many skirmishes and vanquished monsters.

The sound grew as the walls spun faster, making it impossible for them to follow any single archway with their eyes. She knew that once the walls slowed and the spinning stopped, Fate—*or some other power*, Charlotte thought—decided which archway would reveal the next creature they had to defeat.

The battles lasted as long as necessary, and she and Cat won when they either shoved their enemies back into their world or ended their lives on the stone floor, the latter of the two options being their go-to at this point to conserve energy and magic. Exhaustion had her wondering if something different would happen if she or Cat fell, but that wasn't on the table—not as long as she was alive to have anything to say about it.

She and Cat remained still in the center of the chamber as the walls spun around them, light strobing from the flickering archways. The rotation began to slow, and Charlotte held her breath to see which archway would release what creature next. She hoped their next task wouldn't be another battle. More than anything, the fairy godmother wanted to find a way out of there and back to Alex and Sir Thomas, but as things stood, that seemed impossible. For her and Cat, there was no way out, not yet.

When the walls of the chamber finally settled with an almighty boom reverberating through the stone, the fairy godmother and her companion tensed. They scanned the dozens of portals, each potentially harboring new champions sent to challenge the adventurers who had come this far. It seemed an entire lifetime passed before Charlotte noticed any change in the chamber's silence, temperature, or the subtle signs that often preceded an imminent attack.

Nothing, however, could have prepared her for the horror coming through the next portal to open. Fear sent chills down her spine, reminding her of a battle she fought long ago. It had taken an entire group of fairy godmothers to defeat the creature that was so terrifying it had no name.

Her eyes widened as the first of her senses were assaulted with the preliminary warning signs that her memory had not betrayed her. The enchanted cave, or whoever was controlling it, had chosen this creature as the period to end her final chapter because *surely,* there was no way for her and a dog to beat what took an army of fairy godmothers to take down once before.

Cat yipped when he saw the fear on her face, and she knew right away what he wanted to know. He wanted to know what it was. What could have spooked her so severely that she'd no doubt paled.

Swallowing thickly, Charlotte responded.

"The Demon."

CHAPTER FOURTEEN

The low, guttural roar echoing throughout the chamber caused thick clouds of dust and small pebbles to rain down around Charlotte and Cat from the once smooth walls and domed ceilings, now dented and cracked. It was a sound Charlotte Weaver had only heard once before in her lifetime, but once had been more than enough.

The roar bellowing through the archway was unmistakable despite the centuries that had passed since she first heard it at the very beginning of her career as a fairy godmother of the Guild. Charlotte didn't need to see which doorway it was to know that she and Cat were in grave danger.

For the first time since their nearly impossible goal of surviving this chamber without an exit had begun, a cold wave of true terror washed over her.

"This can't be," she whispered, spinning around to lock eyes on the source of that dark, growling cry that had brought her so much pain and regret.

Beside her, Cat crouched low, offering a warning growl

of his own as he also searched for the archway that had opened to them.

When Charlotte finally found the offending portal and the world to which it belonged, everything she remembered about the creature came rushing back to her, and it made sense that the Guild would have banished such a horror to such a place.

Thick, noxious, gray-brown smoke spilled through the shimmering doorway into the chamber in suffocating plumes. When it had cleared enough, she saw a dry, rocky wasteland where the sky was as black as death and great fissures in the earth spewed pillars of fire. It would have been a hellish pit if Charlotte had believed such a place existed, but it was the perfect fit for that nightmarish monster.

Charlotte hadn't felt genuine fear the whole time, locked within the chamber, battling one champion after another. She'd been worried a few times, but never fearful. This, however, changed everything. She'd seen the devastation it could cause, and Charlotte couldn't imagine a worse enemy for her and Cat to face.

It was a beast so ancient, so unholy, so rotten to its core and vicious beyond belief that, within all the texts maintained by the Fairy Godmothers' Guild, it was known only as "The Demon."

Charlotte Weaver did not believe in actual demons as described in stories. None of those stories even came close. But she most certainly believed in *this* Demon. Her only thought was that the only thing she and Cat could do now was to prepare for the end because the end was surely coming for them.

There would be no escape.

The fairy godmother turned to fully face the portal leading into the hellscape of rock, flame, and poisoned sky. Another plume of noxious black smoke churned through the archway, bringing with it the stench of sulfur, decaying meat, and the terror of The Demon's innocent victims. She choked on the thickness of it filling her nostrils, and another bellowing roar rose through the archway, shaking the very foundations of the chamber.

"Cat," Charlotte whispered, "I am so sorry." Her eyes wandered over to him, and though he didn't meet look at her, she saw his ears perked up and knew he was listening. "I've faced this one before. I don't think we'll make it out of this one with our lives."

Her companion did not dignify her words with a response. Instead, he crouched low, ready as ever to fight their next opponent.

He has no idea what this is. He has no idea what we're about to face and how impossible it will be for only the two of us to defeat this thing on our own. We don't have nearly enough power between us. And what stark raving, ignorant lunatic thought to add a doorway to that realm?

Another cold shudder racked her body, but she squared her shoulders to face the oncoming danger. For the first time in her life, Charlotte found herself practically frozen with hopelessness.

But the next second, despite what she knew of this thing, she raised her wand and nodded. "To the end, then. All right, Cat?"

He let out another low growl, and that was all the answer she needed.

She gave a curt nod. They would continue to the very end. They had started this journey together, and they would finish it together, whether by escaping, which now seemed unlikely, or falling to The Demon making its way toward them.

She heard a rumbling bellow and hiss, like an explosion of water powerful enough to turn the entire lake to steam even as flames raged.

That was exactly what The Demon did to entire bodies of water, fields, people, animals—hell, to whole worlds.

All she could do was stare at the open archway as it continued to spew charcoal smoke toward them while the ground rocked and trembled beneath their feet.

This wasn't another earthquake. It was The Demon drawing ever nearer, and the fairy godmother knew the difference.

Another burst of black smoke puffed through the archway and rose to pool in the domed ceiling. It was followed by furious tongues of bright red-orange fire curling around the archway's perimeter, scorching the stone as The Demon finally showed itself on the other side.

The monstrous beast was so impossibly large that Charlotte couldn't fathom how it would fit through the tiny doorway, but she had no doubt it would find a way. Her only hope now was to discover The Demon's weakness that not even the oldest sages, fairy godmothers, or wisest soothsayers of EverAfter had found. Short of that, she and her sweet, furry companion were out of luck.

The chamber trembled again as a crack started to form on her side of the archway. It splintered across the smooth stone floor, riddled with the carcasses of beasts Charlotte and Cat had slain together.

More smoke and even hotter flames with blue at the base spewed through the crevice, forcing Charlotte to leap aside to avoid the fissure racing between her legs. Cat joined her on the same side, and the pair could only watch in horror as The Demon pulled itself free from the deadened world to which it had been banished.

The monster must have been able to change its physical shape and structure because nothing that size could possibly fit through an archway that size but fit it did.

Its form—comprised of smoke, flame, and evil incarnate—billowed and warped in all directions. With all the smoke and fire, it was hard to make out what she was seeing until a limb emerged. As it did, she made out a bony black elbow covered in hard, chitinous armor glinting in the low light.

Her eyes wandered over to discover claws reaching through the cloud of smoke to dig into the stone floor and pull as The Demon scraped its way through the small door and into the chamber.

The Demon's horrifying limbs boasted three or more hands with claws unlike those of regular beasts. Whipping, lashing black tails careened through the smoke, each end held fire so hot their tips could slice through anything this world or any other had to offer. Within that roiling, shifting mass of power and death, Charlotte saw The Demon's eyes.

It was impossible to count how many it had. Dozens, perhaps hundreds, of eyes shifted within the mass of black smoke and flame, and all of them were as red as Charlotte's own blood.

They shifted quickly to peer around the chamber, taking in the sights, the various doorways, and the lifeless carcasses of defeated creatures from more than a dozen other realms.

Then, every single one of those burning blood-red orbs swiveled around at once to fix firmly upon the fairy godmother and the Newfoundland standing heroically beside her with his hackles raised and teeth bared.

Charlotte and Cat were ready to battle again, though this time, only the fairy godmother seemed to realize there would be no coming out of it on the other side.

This is it. Everything I tried to do, everything I still haven't accomplished... My own quest to restore my handbook and return to my world, to confront the Guild and save those betrayed by it. To save EverAfter and Earth from threats— Everyone who still needs my help... After all that, this is how it ends, huh?

And Alex...

The thought of him was too painful to bear. She'd been aware for a while that something special was growing between them, and now, even thinking of it shattered her heart.

So, instead, she centered her attention on Cat and slowly reached down with her free hand to bury her fingers in the soft, fluffy fur of his pitch-black coat.

"It has been an honor to fight by your side, Cat," she said, not once taking her eyes off The Demon crawling toward them as it inched out of the archway. The beast was in no rush because both predator and prey knew there was no escape. "There isn't a fairy godmother, past or present, who could have asked for a better companion. Or a better friend."

Charlotte took another deep breath and fought the urge to cough as the nauseating fumes from The Demon's entrance wormed their way into her lungs. She was grateful the chamber was so tall, and that smoke rose.

"I only have one regret. I wish that I had told Alex—"

A plume of smoke and a horrendous spray of bright, searing flame erupted from the fissure racing through the center of the circular chamber, interrupting what Charlotte thought would be her last words. The Demon let out another terrifying, trembling roar that shook the foundations of the cavern. That same death call had shaken so many other worlds before the Guild banished the beast to a hellscape worthy of it.

But now it was free.

Another growling rumble filled the air as The Demon scraped and clawed its way toward them, but this noise clearly did not come from whatever semblance of a mouth the unholy monster possessed. Neither did it come from the world beyond that open archway or from any other creatures that somehow managed to survive within that realm.

In fact, the rolling rumble was the grating roar of stone grinding against stone, a sound Charlotte and Cat were both quite familiar with.

"What in the hell is—"

In her surprise, Charlotte missed the chance to avert her face from the next bloom of noxious fumes heading her way. Her question ended in a coughing fit, but she couldn't tear her eyes away from what she had discovered.

Amid the chaos caused by the hell beast, Charlotte's heart soared with a flicker of hope. She tried to tamp it down into a semblance of calm and logic.

It can't be. There's no way that this is happening.

The circular walls of the massive chamber had once again begun to spin. The chamber—which was large enough to battle thirteen different species of beasts—now felt much too small for the churning, roiling mass of The Demon's many corporal and ethereal parts. The walls turned faster and faster, just as they had every time Charlotte and Cat had defeated one of their foes in this enclosed arena.

But this time, they hadn't defeated anything.

This time, there seemed no logical reason for the walls to be moving at all.

The hope that dared to well in Charlotte's breast instantly died when she realized what that movement meant.

Oh, no... Please no.

Charlotte couldn't help but believe there was no possible way they could get through this. If she and Cat hadn't had any chance of surviving one monster before, now there was even less of a chance if they needed to defeat The Demon *and* something else. If the hell beast didn't consume them instantly, whatever popped out of one of the open archways next would surely be the end of them.

Despite herself, Charlotte took a quick step backward from The Demon's smoky, fiery form, uncertain where the next archway would open, but certain one would. Wherever it happened to be, she wanted to be as far away from both it and The Demon as possible, and that was becoming more unlikely by the second.

The walls continued to spin, picking up speed until a veritable gust of swirling air swept up The Demon's noxious charcoal fumes, creating a suffocating, deadly maelstrom.

Cat barked madly, his voice hoarse from doing so since they had first entered the chamber, but Charlotte couldn't blame him for making as much noise as he could now. This was their final hour, and the enchanted dog was determined to go out without backing down, despite the fear that gripped the fairy godmother and surely him, too.

Unlike every other time the archways had spun to reveal a new secret world, this time, the walls groaned to a near-instant, clanging stop. Cracks splintered through the previously smooth stone walls. Fire, smoke, and the stench of death and sulfur swirled around the room. From deep within the bowels of the cavern came several clinks, thumps, and resounding booms that sounded like geared mechanisms falling into place.

Confusion washed over Charlotte; she didn't have a clue what was happening. She could hardly see through the smoke and flame, especially when the fissure cutting the chamber in two belched up another burst, blocking her view of the other side.

Something's different. Something changed. This isn't like before.

The timbre and cadence of Cat's nonstop barking changed in an instant. So did the distance between them, which Charlotte realized the second she heard him. She spun around to face her companion and found nothing but more cloudy smoke stinging her nostrils and burning her eyes, making it damn near impossible to see.

"Cat!" she called over The Demon's bellow, the roar of flames, and the clacking booms spreading away from them throughout the bedrock of this magical site between worlds. "Cat, where are you? I can't see you! I—"

She stopped short when Cat gently tugged on her free hand. His mouth was warm, wet, and a little slimy. Usually, the sensation would have made her think twice since she couldn't see for sure what it was, but without a doubt, she knew it was Cat coming to lead her somewhere.

His teeth settled firmly but gently around her hand. With her heart pounding in her ears and her lungs near to bursting with toxic fumes and a lack of breathable oxygen, Charlotte closed her eyes and let her companion do what he had come back for. She trusted wholly in Cat's ability to lead her because, after all they had been through today, he had not led her awry.

She stumbled through the smoke and the searing heat clawing at her dark purple cloak and violet dress. The smell clung to her hair, the heat prickled her flesh, and the smoke shoved itself down her throat and made it impossible to tell left from right and up from down. Hell, she wasn't even entirely sure any longer if she was alive or dead. The fumes had left her dizzy and confused.

Somewhere behind her, The Demon let out another furious bellow, which was followed instantly by a searing heat whizzing past her head inches above her right shoulder. An explosion crashed into the wall up ahead and to her right, blasting the same heat back at her face. It sent her fight or flight instinct into overdrive, making everything inside her scream to pull her hand away, turn tail, and run in the opposite direction, though she was well aware that The Demon was waiting for her.

Somehow, she let Cat lead her onward. Then he stopped without warning and released her hand from his gentle grasp.

Blinking the tears, burning heat, and poisoned air out of her eyes, Charlotte managed to catch a glimpse of something through her blurry vision. Something tall and rounded at the top in front of her. Something dark without the blaze of fire, unmarred by burns and blackened fumes.

Something that released a gloriously cool breath of fresh air right into her face, and it did not smell of terror and her own demise.

The fairy godmother sucked in a raw, painful breath of fresh air to clear out her lungs. The hope in that single breath jerked her out of her despair, clearing her mind while also bringing more tears to her eyes because she recognized this feeling.

It was a relief. It was hope that she and Cat still had one final, infinitesimal chance.

Charlotte stepped forward, her ears ringing with The Demon's deadly call and the whistling whip of hot air and flame searing across the chamber toward her.

Her honed senses kicked in, and she knew without having to look that the whistling wind was a fireball or some other type of explosion heading toward her. She knew this even before the warning heat of the blast reached her body, and if she didn't move, Cat had risked his life to rescue her for nothing.

The fairy godmother dropped into a crouch and threw herself forward with all her might, gossamer wings shimmering and fluttering madly to add an extra burst of speed. Cat barked wildly from somewhere in front of her.

Charlotte's chest, stomach, and hips hit cool, solid stone that didn't seem to have any enormous fissures tearing through it. The ground felt so incredibly refreshing that she wanted nothing more than to press her cheek against it, savoring the sweet coolness that smelled like minerals and earth.

But she was fully aware of the danger, and with Cat's continuous barking to remind her, the fairy godmother scrambled onto her hands and knees and launched herself forward again. She thumped into something solid, perhaps a stone on the ground or some other obstacle she didn't have time to identify. After toppling over the unknown object, she crashed face-first onto the ground again and struggled to rise.

Behind her, The Demon let out another screeching bellow, and pillars of flame shot toward her. Their agonizing heat intensified by the second, and the rumbling groan of the chamber walls spinning overpowered every other noise within Charlotte's awareness.

This time, the grinding of stone moving against stone seemed to last forever. As she lay on the floor, the cool stone was now beneath her cheek because she no longer had the strength to pick herself up. Not yet.

A lifetime seemed to pass before the spinning stone walls ground to an abrupt halt, booming and clanking all around her. The way it sounded, Charlotte wouldn't have been surprised to find herself within the bowels of the cave, lying in front of some enormous turning, churning stone mechanism responsible for all the confusion and horrors she and Cat had endured.

Still, she did not get up.

The echoes of those unknown, unseen mechanisms grinding to a halt finally died down, and then everything around Charlotte was nothing but pure, utter, blessed silence.

When she could hold her breath no longer, she puffed it all out in a massive sigh that almost made her jump out of her own skin. Even after everything, her own sigh sounded ear-shatteringly loud. She recovered slightly, however, and took another deep breath before deciding on anything else.

You have to look, Charlotte. You have to see where you are. You have to make sure Cat's okay and if this is real and not some dream or the afterlife because you're unconscious or your body's currently being mangled to bits between The Demon's monstrous jaws. You have to keep going!

It was enough to get her moving again, despite how much she wanted to keep lying there on the cold stone floor, breathing fresh air, with all her body parts seemingly still intact.

With a grunt of effort, Charlotte pushed herself up off the floor with shaky arms to a sitting position and finally opened her eyes. When she turned to look behind her to see where The Demon was so she could plan her next move, a gasp escaped her.

Her eyes widened as the sight of a solid stone wall greeted her. Tears once again filled her eyes before spilling onto her cheeks, but these weren't from pain. They were from the realization that the cave had opened a door for them, which Cat had led them through.

We did it. We passed. Maybe this is a quest cave, after all. Her mind spun for a few seconds.

"How the hell did we get out with the walls spinning?" she breathed.

An archway appeared that wasn't part of the spinning walls, Cat whined.

"Oh." It was all Charlotte had the energy or brain power to process. *Magical cave. Magical walls. Why wouldn't a random door just materialize out of nowhere?*

Looking around, she discovered she was in a new corridor, but that wasn't the only thing she saw. Another gasp escaped her when she noticed something she had long forgotten about with all the chaos—a page from her handbook.

They had finally made it. Everything they had endured —all the exhaustion, confusion, terror, and self-doubt— had led to this moment.

Without hesitation, Charlotte inspected the newly retrieved page of her handbook, folded it, and gingerly tucked it into the hidden folds of her cloak, and nodded at the path ahead, lit brilliantly for its newest adventurers.

Her mind wandered briefly to Alex, and more tears spilled. Her time wasn't up. She still had a chance.

Whoever is listening to prayers out there, thank you.

CHAPTER FIFTEEN

Charlotte stood in the long, well-lit corridor that symbolized life and freedom to her, even though they were still trapped within the cave. Now that the chamber had spat them out and separated them from The Demon, essentially letting them go free, staring down the stone hallway felt like looking toward what very much seemed like Fate.

"I really wish Alex was here right now to see all this." She let out an unamused laugh. "Though I must say, I'm glad he wasn't around to see The Demon. That would be too much for any human to bear, but he's always been particularly grumpy about magic." She smiled as she thought about how he grumbled over it sometimes. "That just might have been the thing that broke our poor detective."

Her smile faltered. *It was nearly enough to break* me, *and I'd seen that hell spawn before.*

She shivered as a cold chill raced through her at the thought of what could have happened in that room. Beside her, the enormous, shaggy black dog let out a low whine and licked his chops.

Sir Thomas, too!

Her smile returned, still grateful she could understand him, though for how long, she didn't know. "Of course," she replied, looking down at her furry companion with a calm smile. "Sir Thomas, too. I wish they could both be here. Hell, I wish it wasn't just you and me continuing through the rest of this quest without them. At least this part of it anyway."

Charlotte sighed and shook her head before taking another slow breath and blowing it out to help her lungs. The fairy godmother's chest was still tight from the smoke damage, and she had a feeling the only reason she was standing was thanks to the fact she was a magical being and could, therefore, handle a bit more damage than the average human.

I don't think Alex would have made it out with all those fumes. The thought entered her head, and she quickly shook it away. She couldn't bear to think of such things.

"We've been through so much together already, and honestly, I'm glad they missed out on all that danger. It was hard enough to keep track of you. I can't imagine how difficult it would have been to watch over all three of you. I trust Sir Thomas. He's strong and quick, both physically and in wit, but his senses seem much more normal for a bipedal EverAfteran cat. Yours, however, seem to give you precognitive abilities. You seem to know things before they happen, so I didn't have to worry so much about you."

Charlotte stretched her arms over her head, trying to work some of the tension out of her side where she'd been injured and in her body as a whole. She recalled seeing signs throughout Cincinnati advertising massages, and she wondered if she might be able to coax Alex into gifting her a session.

She hated feeling like a mooch, but after all this, she *needed* to heal, and that sounded like a logical first step. Well, maybe the logical *second* step, right after her three scalding hot showers, a week of sleep, a pound of chocolate, a bottle of wine, and binge-watching her favorite shows.

I wish they'd been here with us. Sir Thomas would have loved all those battles, even if he complained the whole time, Cat whined with a little yip at the end.

Charlotte reached down for her toes, wincing as her side doubled over.

"I know, buddy. It's a little unfair that they had to sit and wait for us in that giant cavern where we left them, not to mention Alex is completely unconscious. He missed out on this whole incredible journey, and he'll miss out on the rest if we can't figure out a way to wake him from whatever sleeping spell he has gotten himself into. I know he'll be upset because as much as Alex hates magic, I think there's a spot deep down that gets excited about it. He seemed more than a little interested in the prospect of a quest cave, and I'm sure he was curious to see real magic. Unfortunately, things don't always go as planned. We had to do what we had to do, my friend."

We need to go, Lady Charlotte. Cat let out a low chuff before nudging his cold, wet snout gently against her thigh.

She looked back at the long passageway extending before them. There for a while, she'd started to question if this was an enchanted quest cave at all or if someone had simply lured and trapped her and her companions while slowly trying to kill them off.

Now that she and Cat had successfully made it through the roster of chosen champions—minus The Demon—she was far more convinced this was, indeed, a quest cave. Even if it didn't follow the rules. Still, knowing this was finally part of their official sacred quest renewed her sense of adventure and gave her a bit of energy, too.

"I know, I know," she said, chuckling despite herself at Cat's prodding. "I'm as ready as I'll ever be, especially with another page of my spell book right here. With how many dots I saw on the map before we entered the cave, I feel most of them are right here. I initially thought they were surrounding Ginger's cottage, but now I realize the map was reading this cave, *not* the witch's land.

"With this one safe and sound and tucked away until I need it, I plan to find the others in here. Actually, if I can find the specific missing page I've been looking for, there's a spell in the book to find cherished things lost and long forgotten. Obviously, the pages are not long forgotten, but they *are* cherished and certainly lost. I don't know if it will work, but I figured it's worth a try."

If I'm finding pages here in this place, what better sign that this is exactly where I'm supposed to be right now? There isn't, she thought.

Cat was ready to get this show on the road, but Charlotte needed a few minutes more. Her lungs and eyes still burned mercilessly. Talking helped, forcing her to breathe, and kept the antsy dog occupied while she burned time recovering.

I can't figure out how he *hasn't collapsed on the floor. Enchanted or not, he's still an Earth dog. He should be just as limited as any other creature here,* she pondered.

She looked back down at Cat to inspect him for any signs he might be hiding his symptoms but saw nothing aside from a sense of adventure and excitement in his eyes. He looked like a normal Earth dog when its owners asked if he wanted to go for a walk. His eyes glistened with readiness.

"What about you?" she asked. "Are you feeling okay? You seem fine, but I need to know if you're ready for this. Rest is just as important as the adventure. If your eyes and lungs hurt like mine, maybe a few more minutes wouldn't hurt."

He looked up at her with those enormous brown eyes, his tongue lolling from the side of his mouth. Charlotte would have taken that as a yes, but a muted, furious bellow from the chamber beyond momentarily distracted them. Even through the stone walls, the call was no less terrifying.

Charlotte and Cat's eyes darted toward the now perfectly solid wall. Despite knowing several feet of thick, solid stone separated them, she also knew the cave had a habit of changing at a moment's notice. Not to mention, the beast inside that chamber was a world-ender. A few feet of stone was nothing.

We really *need to get out of here. I think that thing can hear us,* Cat whined again softly.

After eyeing the solid stone wall between them and the otherworldly creature still rampaging on the other side, Charlotte pressed her lips together and then nodded. "As much as I'd like to know what's to become of that thing, The Demon still sounds pretty pissed. Probably because we narrowly escaped becoming its lunch or dinner or whatever. I'm just terrified that thing will escape. If this were a regular cave, I'd be more anxious. However, since it's magical, hopefully the magic inside is enough to—"

Another bellow cut her off, followed by a violent rumble within the chamber. A trembling *boom* came from the other side, and loose dust and small rocks rained down around the fairy godmother and her companion. Her eyes widened as she leaped back, nearly stumbling over her own feet.

Charlotte, I'm strong enough to drag you by that cloak, Cat snorted and shook his head, one forepaw lifted in readiness to flee.

"Uh, yep. Sorry. You said it. Time for us to get a move on." She gestured forward for Cat to lead the way. She didn't want to risk talking again, wondering if The Demon really could still hear them speaking, thus sending it into a rage when it couldn't reach its prey. *"Run,"* she mouthed, and Cat responded by quickly navigating around random rocks and rubble lying about the tunnel.

The Newfoundland had padded paws and long fur between the pads to dampen his steps even more, though the tiny clicks of his claws gave him away. Charlotte, however, had on boots, and there would be no running in those without potentially making enough noise to send The Demon into a bigger rage.

So, instead, she opted to use the wings she'd missed so much before this latest adventure. *They need the exercise anyway,* she thought.

With her wand gripped tightly, Charlotte flew through the corridor, following her trusty companion, who always seemed to know where to go. The thrashing within the chamber grew quieter as they hurried away. At the same time, the more distance they put between them and the chamber of horrors, the more focused she became. She felt far more energized and optimistic than she had mere minutes ago.

Once the banging and thrashing were no longer within earshot, they slowed, and she lowered herself to stand on the stone floor. The moment her feet touched down, she realized just how much they hurt. Even the thought of walking made her feel nauseated, but she pushed it aside. Using magic to boost her wasn't an option. She couldn't risk using even the tiniest of spells now that she'd seen what could happen when she wasn't ready.

Charlotte tossed loose hair out of her eyes and swiped sweat and blood from her cheek and neck. The wound from the crow stung, but it had already scabbed over, which meant it was healing. It was small enough that a slight infection would be easy for her to heal later. The one on her side wouldn't have been quite as easy to heal, which was why she'd needed to close it immediately.

The fairy godmother followed her companion, jumping slightly with each step. There was no way to tell where this new path would lead, but she hoped it would get them out of there soon. After surviving everything they'd faced in that room, her biggest goal was to get back to Alex. Charlotte truly believed she'd die before ever getting the chance to tell him how she felt, and she wouldn't make that same mistake twice.

Thinking of Alex made her wonder how they were doing. While she had faith in Sir Thomas' ability to keep himself and Alex safe, Charlotte did not trust the inner workings of this cave. For all she knew, the doorway she and Cat had narrowly escaped through might open at the last second, letting The Demon into the corridor.

Then they'd be chased down and killed with flames and toxic smoke filling their lungs while the hell spawn bellowed triumphantly.

You can't let yourself think like that, Charlotte. Move on. You and Cat made it through. Leave The Demon and all those other creatures behind where they belong. She sighed as she reminded herself this wouldn't have turned out like it did if it wasn't safe for her to leave. *If this enchanted cavern could summon it, it's capable of putting that thing back where it belongs and protecting innocents.*

Like many others Charlotte had encountered while guiding heroes on their adventures, this cave was almost sentient. It existed within sacred magical sites that lay between realms and seemed to think for itself. Charlotte had to trust that this one was no different, even though it had challenged her and Cat in ways she hadn't anticipated.

She and Cat had escaped with their lives, which was the greatest prize any adventurer could hope for. And finally, Charlotte had recovered another page of her handbook, one of the more powerful and dangerous pages in her collection.

The Hidden Sundering spell. Fairy godmothers were only supposed to use it as a last resort and under no other circumstances. If that wasn't an ace up her sleeve, she didn't know what was.

At that moment, Charlotte felt as if everything had suddenly started to look up for her and Cat. Even the corridor they now journeyed through seemed to reflect this sentiment.

The curved ceiling was at least four feet higher than any other tunnel in the cave so far. The walls were wider apart. Charlotte couldn't touch either side as she walked down the center beside Cat with her arms spread wide.

For the first time since entering the cave, she didn't need to summon one of her own illumination orbs. The corridor was already lit in a way Charlotte found surprisingly pleasant. Torches were set in sconces along the wall, casting a warm, inviting yellow-orange glow that flickered as they passed.

The sconces lined both walls, alternating sides every ten feet to provide ample light. The flames remained steady as Charlotte and Cat walked, and no new torches ignited ahead. Charlotte couldn't see the end of the corridor yet, but everything about this passageway indicated that things finally were as they should be.

This corridor seemed meant for the fairy godmother and her furry companion. They seemed more welcome here, encouraged to continue onward as far as their determination, courage, and loyalty to their cause would take them.

A swell of pride bloomed in Charlotte's chest as she shot Cat a quick, knowing look. "Something tells me that you and I are almost there, my friend."

He sniffed at the air, glanced briefly her way, and continued trotting along. *Maybe. There are a lot of confusing smells to sort through in here.*

The fact that Cat found nothing particularly interesting or worthy of his full attention felt important, especially since they had separated from the other half of their small party. Charlotte had enjoyed having ample opportunity to get to know the enchanted dog.

The once average, run-of-the mill Earth cat had been a dog for the entirety of their friendship except for the first two minutes of riding the same bus together. It was then that the fairy godmother's attempt to stop a robbery, mixed with the unpredictability of using magic in Cincinnati, Ohio, transformed a tired street cat sleeping under the bus seat into the formidable canine Cat had become.

Charlotte had experienced a rapid and deep connection with her furry friend during their latest trials in this cave. She knew beyond a shadow of a doubt that she could depend on him to do whatever was necessary to achieve their goals. She trusted him with her life and had done so more than once during their brief time questing alone together.

Despite Cat's lack of verbal language abilities, like those of Sir Thomas, the fairy godmother no longer had to wonder what Cat might have thought or felt. While she couldn't be totally sure what had happened to allow her to understand her companion, she had a strong feeling it was because they'd established a real bond between them during their battles with the otherworldly creatures in the spinning chamber.

While understanding Cat hadn't been on Charlotte's list of goals, mostly because she never believed it was possible, she no longer found it odd that she had gained the ability to communicate with him at a level previously reserved for Sir Thomas.

When they reached the first bend in the corridor, Cat's reaction didn't faze the fairy godmother in the slightest. She barely noticed when he dipped his head closer to the stone floor, sniffed the air a few times, then stretched his snout toward the bend and let out a low, barely audible woof that didn't echo.

I can't tell what's ahead yet, but something's there.

Charlotte chuckled softly. "Well, not even *you* can know *everything*, my friend. This is a long tunnel. I'm sure the next will be just as long or longer. If you can't smell anything specific yet, that's probably a good thing. I wouldn't worry about it too much if I were you. Something tells me this is nothing like the archway chamber."

It sure as hell better not be, she thought to herself.

I hope you're right, Cat whined, closely echoing her own sentiments.

Still, she couldn't completely discard his warning. He had sensed something up ahead, even if he didn't know enough to say what it was. Charlotte had no more insight into the matter than he did, but his warning was a gentle reminder that they were not out of the woods yet—or out of the cave, to be specific.

"Thank you for bringing it to my attention," she added, lowering her voice despite suspecting they were still alone.

Even though only one of her three companions was currently with her, Charlotte had no doubt she and Cat would reunite with Sir Thomas and Alex after completing their part of the quest.

Remaining positive was crucial. Charlotte Weaver was

not the type to view the world through a pessimistic lens. Optimism had always been one of her strengths, sometimes even to her detriment, and she never let it overpower her sense of logic when working to achieve her goals.

Right now, she and Cat needed to finish their portion of the quest, which meant dealing with whatever awaited them at the end of this corridor. As they traveled along, she couldn't help but think that this was exactly the type of corridor Charlotte had expected them to find from the beginning when they first entered the quest cave.

Everything happens for a reason, especially in a place like this. That is the most important thing to remember.

Far more attuned now to Cat's awareness and the way he slowed to a conscious prowl as they rounded another bend, Charlotte echoed her companion's caution and slowed as well.

What she did not expect was to see the cozy line of flaming torches on the wall end around the curve in the corridor. The fairy godmother couldn't tell right away where this corridor had led them. The vastness beyond where the tunnel ended, and a new chamber began was much darker, with no torches or flames of any type to provide warmth and light in a place that felt so cold and confusing.

Cat took a few careful steps forward and chuffed. *There's a sharp drop here, so be careful.*

"Like a '*dead-end*' kind of drop or a '*we need to get creative*' kind of drop?" she asked softly, following Cat's lead with the volume. If he wanted to avoid his usual whines, which tended to carry, then she needed to be quieter as well.

Staying low, she crept forward and crouched beside Cat as they came to the very end of the corridor and the edge of a sharp drop into the cavern beyond. The fairy godmother hunkered down on all fours beside Cat, who crouched low to peer over the drop to view what lay before them. His tail was tucked slightly between his legs in apprehension, and his ears perked while his brown eyes took in everything.

Charlotte squinted as she studied what she could of this next chamber, though it was far darker than she had expected. After having ample light for so long, it would take a bit longer for her vision to adjust to the lack of it.

She lifted her wand slightly when she first thought to toss more orbs into the air, but then she paused at the same time Cat's paw gently pressed down on her wrist.

We don't know what's down there yet. Wait.

While she'd only just come to that conclusion herself, she merely nodded and lowered her hand once again.

Well, this certainly throws a hammer in things, or whatever Alex says, she thought.

Before she could even think of using any spells to conjure light that would immediately give their position away to anything lurking below, she needed to wait until her vision adjusted to the semi-darkness. As it slowly did, she mentally cataloged everything visible from their perch on top of this veritable cliff.

While Charlotte trusted her own instincts, she trusted Cat's far more in this situation, and she was more interested in knowing what he would find than what she could. At the moment, her biggest concern was how she and Cat were supposed to get off that ledge to successfully complete what she was certain remained the last phase of her quest.

She had wings, of course, so she would be fine. And there was always the option for her to use her magic to bubble them and carry him along as she had earlier in the fight with the Kraken, but she was feeling quite stingy with her magic.

Not to mention, they were far higher in the air. If the cave decided Charlotte shouldn't have complete control of her magic anymore, Cat could plummet to his death.

She had a feeling this might take a minute to process and plan, but she was confident this was just another random test of wits, and she needed to comply.

CHAPTER SIXTEEN

It took longer than Charlotte would have liked for her eyes to adjust to the darkness below, but when it did, she was able to assess their situation better.

The first thing she noticed about this new chamber was feeling like they'd stumbled upon somewhere far more ancient and powerful than anywhere else in the quest cave. The only thing she'd seen so far that compared was the ancient dark forest where the entrance to the cave stood, and this seemed even older than that somehow. There was something here that whispered of the past, of a time lost to memory and history itself.

It felt like Charlotte and Cat were crouching on the precipice of a chamber of time, where one misstep might send them tumbling back through decades, centuries, or even millennia before they could figure out what had happened. The fairy godmother attributed that overpowering sensation to what this new chamber contained.

Far larger than the previous chamber, with its rotating walls and portal doors into dozens of different worlds, this chamber was also far older. The walls and floor were lumpy instead of uniform, as if they had either been dug away or had set here for incomprehensible lengths of time to be eaten away by time—like the oldest tombstones in a cemetery that were so weather-beaten that they no longer bore much resemblance to their original shape.

The ceiling, however, was remarkably high, stretching far above even where Charlotte and Cat were perched at the edge of the ledge until it almost couldn't be seen. Its surface was smooth and seemingly crafted from a single piece of stone chiseled away from within.

Dim illumination came from enormous stone pieces set at varying intervals along the chamber floor. These hulking monoliths of solid rock were carved into the shape of obelisks, three feet wide at the bottom and growing narrower as they rose toward the ceiling. Charlotte counted six in all.

Though she couldn't be sure due to the lack of light, it seemed each of those obelisks had been crafted from a different type of stone. One had a rosy hue, another had a milky white sheen, and yet another had an occasional glimpse of violet reflecting off its surface when Charlotte shifted her head. The material of the other three was more challenging to figure out from where she crouched, though she could see their colors.

All six held their own internal glow with a slightly tinted hue unique to each. Though there didn't seem to be a true pattern or meaning for their placement, they were equally interspersed between larger boulders with carvings etched into their sides.

It was impossible to see it all from the fairy godmother's vantage point on the ledge, but someone—or something—had placed the central piece in the chamber quite purposefully. That was precisely where Charlotte's gaze was drawn over and over as she put the pieces together in her mind of what this new chamber could be.

The structure in the center of the chamber was simple in design and, therefore, most likely simple in purpose, too. It was a solid stone slab carved into a rough rectangle, though its surface seemed perfectly leveled and sanded to a smooth, glinting sheen. It appeared to be some sort of table without legs, perhaps even etched out of the very foundations of this magical earth within the quest cave.

That's an altar if I've ever seen one, which makes me worry about exactly what this place was used for. I didn't come here to make the kind of sacrifices people used tables like that for.

The fairy godmother tried to keep those thoughts to herself, knowing that worrying about unconfirmed fears was a waste of time and energy. Not to mention, she knew working herself up into a fit of anxiety before they figured out what they were supposed to do here wouldn't be the best of ideas. It was a distraction at best and held the possibility of getting them killed at worst.

The stone table in the center was the only monument there that did not contain its own internal glow like the obelisks. As Charlotte continued to look around, she noticed the table kept inexplicably drawing her attention despite it not being the new chamber's most astonishing feature.

That title belonged to the single proof of life in this part of the cave, though "life" seemed far too simple of a word for it. It must have held true power to survive down here despite the harsh conditions. No other plant life or vegetation grew within these walls due to the lack of natural sunlight and water.

But Charlotte had a feeling that a monumental force such as the gargantuan tree before them did not have much need for such things or the companionship of other plant life.

The towering tree was far older, taller, and thicker than any that existed within the ancient forest outside the mouth of the questing cave, and it had grown to be part of the cave itself. It was even larger and more impressive than any she had seen in the vast and varied EverAfteran forests or any other lands she had occasionally visited. If she had known about Earth's redwood forests in California, the fairy godmother would have found even those natural giants paling in comparison to this tree.

The trunk reached all the way up toward the chamber ceiling, far above Charlotte and Cat's heads. No branches were visible this far beneath the surface. When she craned her neck to follow the height of the tree, it looked like it had grown all the way through the ceiling of the chamber, perhaps even sprouting ancient leaves somewhere aboveground.

I wonder if this is one of the trees we saw before coming in and just assumed it was normal among the others, she thought.

However, unlike the crown, the tree's roots did not hide themselves nearly as much. They were as thick and wide as Charlotte would have expected from the branches of a living behemoth like this, though much of the root system remained beneath the uneven floor of the chamber.

A significant portion had burst forth from underground to reveal themselves to the cool, dry air. They bent and bowed, arcing up to form natural archways and bridges behind the stone table in the center of the chamber.

Several narrower roots stretched across the open space to dig themselves deeply into the earthen walls behind the tree at the far end of the chamber, like many fingers burrowing into the earth to grab hold and never let go.

This tree stands a good chance of being even older than some of the elder godmothers who trained me. This chamber definitely is.

Mine. I'm gonna pee on that tree, Cat chuffed, drawing her attention.

Her eyes widened and snapped in his direction. When his mouth opened and his tongue lolled out to the side, his jowls lifting at the corners in what appeared to be a smile, the fairy godmother relaxed.

"You nearly gave me a heart attack," she whispered before smiling.

He panted in response. *Dog humor. They pee on everything.*

She quirked a brow. "Sir, I don't know if you know this, but you are, in fact, a dog now."

And whose fault is that?

She looked at him incredulously. "Fair point. Also... rude. Also-also, to your joke... Not funny."

He leaned over and licked the back of her wand hand to apologize. *You looked tense. I thought you could use a bit of humor.*

Reaching over, Charlotte scratched just behind his ears,

where he always seemed to like it most. "Thanks for looking out for me, buddy."

As Charlotte continued to look out over the incredible chamber, she couldn't help but wonder what all this was supposed to mean or how these things had gotten down here in the first place. The answers to those questions were likely useless to what they needed to do, but curiosity had a death grip on her. This site was fascinating, to say the least.

Fate and magic created quest caves exactly as they should be. Places like these were nearly as old as time, making even a member of the Fairy Godmothers' Guild seem insignificant. It practically made Charlotte feel like a baby, which she found remarkably entertaining.

That did not, however, mean she lacked respect for such an ancient site.

It was places like this that birthed the beginning of magic, worlds, creatures, and people. These places existed beyond time and held all the secret knowledge of all the worlds that ever were or ever would be.

Most of that knowledge would remain here for eternity, never leaving the cool, dark confines of this chamber with its strange stone table at the center and the enormous tree growing up through the rear, likely connected to the very lifeblood of this place from before the beginning.

Some secrets, however, were meant to be discovered and shared, which Charlotte believed was the reason Fate had led her and Cat to this chamber. An essential part of their quest existed here, and it was her job to discover what it was and follow the instructions for completing it to the letter.

For less crucial quests—where adventurers sought

fame, glory, or solutions to defeating mythical beasts—answers and directions were freely given. Sometimes, it was all spelled out with a simple plan and a few actionable steps. For Charlotte and her companions, however, the quest was a lot more complicated, making the required steps equally convoluted.

Be that as it may, there was no stopping Charlotte and Cat now. Not after everything they had been through to get there, even if it meant finding a way to scale the side of this cliff from where they perched at the end of the most recent corridor.

One way or another, Charlotte Weaver would see this through, no matter what it took or how long it took, which she hoped wouldn't be much longer. Sir Thomas and Alex were still waiting for her and Cat to return. She knew the swashbuckling cat would expect her to be triumphant and victorious, perhaps even returning with an extra tool, clue, or boon from the Fate that governed magic and all quests.

We need to get started. We won't finish a damn thing if Cat and I keep crouching here at the top of a cliff while all the good stuff is down there, she thought.

Now that she was a bit more confident about what lay below, she began looking around for anything that would serve as a way to get down. A hidden tunnel. A path carved into the side of the cliff. A bridge wrapping around the walls leading down. A pulley system. She didn't care what it was; she just needed to find it.

"Do you see a way down?" she asked Cat. "I *can* use magic, but I'd prefer not to. If we get into trouble down there, I'll need every ounce of power I have left. We've been through a lot with very little rest."

Cat's jaws fell open again as he panted. *I've been looking, but I haven't found anything yet. What about your wings? Are you strong enough to carry me while flying?*

She shook her head and kept her voice low as she spoke. "You're nearly two hundred pounds, big guy. Even bigger than the average Newfie if what Alex told me is correct. There's no way I could carry you on foot, and my wings are out of shape. You have to remember, I haven't flown at all in months."

His mouth closed, and he huffed through his nose. *Good point.*

Without a word, the fairy godmother lowered herself to her belly, still cautious about making sudden moves or loud noises, and poked her chin over the edge for an unobstructed view of the drop to the chamber floor.

It was high, all right. It was easily a seven or eight-story drop, if not more, which wasn't exactly jumping height.

Charlotte once again thought about her wings and how they'd felt to her earlier. She'd used them quite a bit in the chamber, and they'd felt unsteady, but she didn't have any problems. Once they'd escaped The Demon, and Cat led them out into the new tunnel, she'd used them again, and without a battle distracting her, she noticed how heavy she felt while using them.

Her body was just as lean as it always had been, primarily due to walking all over the city with Sir Thomas and Cat to find pages in her handbook. It kept her moving. However, Alex *did* tell her that the food in his world was far unhealthier than the natural stuff grown in hers. Maybe she'd gained a few pounds.

She shook her head. *It doesn't matter. I don't even know if my wings will support* me *for that distance. A fifteen-ish-foot drop upon wing failure in the first chamber during a battle with a Kraken or a four-foot fall in a tunnel is one thing. A seventy-foot* plummet *is something else entirely.*

I can't risk it with him.

Magic worked here in the cave, but once they'd completed the quest, and they made it through every stage, there was no guarantee that it would continue to behave correctly. It could vary at a moment's notice, and it made her uneasy, to say the least.

Charlotte and her companions would still have to return to Cincinnati to ensure Alex got home safe and sound, and that would require a *lot* of magic. Then came the journey home to EverAfter. The fairy godmother suspected they had a lot of work to do before she could leave the human world to confront the Fairy Godmothers' Guild.

Would Alex want to go with her? Would Cat? If so, how would she get them home if she couldn't recover her magic?

There was also the matter of her scattered handbook. Charlotte still had yet to recover all the dispersed pages of her Fairy Godmother's Handbook from wherever they had landed within Cincinnati and even within this cave.

Unless she found the spell page that she needed to locate cherished things lost and forgotten, she had a feeling those pages wouldn't reveal themselves all at once at the end. That had happened once before, and the results had been useless once Miraval, the Gatekeeper, snatched up her handbook and scattered it again before he was obliterated.

She shook her head. Once again, she was worrying herself into a panic. There were too many what-ifs, and she didn't need to focus on those.

Cliff. Chamber. That's it. Nothing else exists right now. Get it together, Charlotte, she scolded herself.

Charlotte and her companions had quite a bit farther to go before reaching the end of their journey together, with much more to accomplish. The adventurer in her was eager to see it through as quickly as possible.

The woman in her, who found something special in a man like Alex, selfishly hoped it took as long as possible.

A low, contemplative hum escaped the fairy godmother as she once again studied the drop over the edge of the cliff. It fell right on top of a seventh stone pillar glowing with its own internal light, which she had not seen within the chamber until now.

"It seems our options are rather limited, Cat," she whispered. "Hey, I could always fly, and you could always jump. Cats always land on their feet, right?"

Cat's large head slowly rotated so he could eye her incredulously, and she almost laughed at the very human gesture.

"Sorry. Cat humor. You looked stressed. I thought you could use it." She winked.

His jaw fell open as he panted again. *Very funny. Also, this large, dumpy body of mine sometimes fails to jump properly off the couch. Dogs are very clumsy beasts. That's what I miss most about being a cat, though I will say the size and strength are a big bonus to being a dog.*

Charlotte shrugged. "That's a good point. As far as magical mishaps go, you got a great end of the deal. After

all, I could have turned you into a corgi...or a chihuahua."
Cat snorted in response, and she chuckled under her
breath. "If you'd been a corgi, we could have taken you to
the groomer and had them shave your rear end into a little
heart like we saw—"

Quiet, Cat cut her off with a low whine. Charlotte
recognized the gentle warning instantly, not even needing
to translate it, and pushed herself back from the edge to
look at him directly.

"I *am* being quiet," she whispered, frowning at Cat. He
remained crouched low on the ledge, his belly pressed to
the stone and his ears flat against his head. "You've been up
here whining, and that carries more than whisp—"

The canine cut her off by nipping at her forearm. He
didn't actually bite her, but the nudge with his snout was
more urgent than ever before.

Her eyes widened, and only a heartbeat after his wet
nose pressed painfully into her shoulder, an unexpected
boom rose from below in the chamber. Her head jerked in
that direction, and she heard more noises alongside the
boom's echo, forming a sharp, rhythmic click on the stone
that grew louder with every successive beat.

*Either that's the sound of our next challenge, or someone's
down there right now. But who could possibly be here? This is a
damn quest cave. Isn't it?*

Without seeing whatever was below, she began to question the validity of the cave once again. If someone was
down there, was that someone the person responsible for
everything that had happened to them? Or were they just
the next part of the adventurer's quest?

The rhythmic click and clack continued before dying

down by the second. Charlotte caught a hint of movement below. She held perfectly still, slowing her breaths to remain as silent as possible. The fairy godmother and her furry companion cautiously peered over the ledge together, side by side, to watch the unexpected activity below.

A dark shape came into view at the bottom of the cliff where Charlotte and Cat crouched. It had already been in the chamber but remained invisible until it moved into the open center. There, six of the seven stone obelisks were visible, along with the massive stone slab of a table and the ancient, twisted tree growing through the back wall.

The figure moved at a purposeful pace, neither hurried nor hesitant. Charlotte quickly realized that the rhythmic sound she'd heard was shoes striking the stone floor. An instant wave of frigid air wafted up from the edge of the cliff, giving her a chill, and she thought she heard the creaking and snapping of water instantly freezing.

As the figure below continued toward the stone table, a trail of glittering frost stretched in its wake, coating the chamber floor in swirling, curly-cue designs. Her jaw fell slightly open as she watched, unsure she fully believed what she was seeing.

The chamber was too large for one figure to affect the entire area, leaving half covered in frost and the other half untouched. But for the cold snap filling the air, Charlotte didn't need to see the figure's face to know who it was. She had seen this kind of destruction in someone's mere presence only once before.

How in all the worlds did the Ice Queen get in here?

A harsh bitterness rose in the back of Charlotte's throat

as she struggled to comprehend the sight before her. The Ice Queen being there was one thing. She and her companions had battled the woman once before. But to see such a villain here in what Charlotte had believed to be the final cavern in her uniquely personal quest was incomprehensible.

This doesn't make any sense. I would say it's impossible, but she's right there. What is she doing? she wondered.

The Ice Queen wore a dark cloak with a heavy cowl that obscured her face. Even when she reached the stone table, stepped behind it, and delicately placed her hands on its smooth, surface, trails of shimmering frost rippled away from her fingers.

For a moment, she held perfectly still, waiting for something. Charlotte still couldn't see the Ice Queen's face, but that hardly mattered. She just wanted to know what the frosty creature was up to, what she was thinking, and most importantly, what she was planning.

Every time Charlotte encountered the Ice Queen, the woman's incredible power was undeniable, but she hadn't mastered her emotions. They could be read in her expressions as easily as words in a book.

That was something many of EverAfter's villains had in common, Charlotte had discovered. They were often unable to mask their desires, fears, doubts, and intentions. Very few had perfected the kind of stony mask that made for a truly formidable villain.

Charlotte supposed that choosing to become a villain often stemmed from heartache, fear, and rage, making it difficult to hide their inner turmoil. Controlling the dark energy that fueled nearly all the villains she'd encountered was the most challenging part of all. It was that lack of control that made EverAfterans like Prince Repel and the Ice Queen so unnervingly dangerous.

Still, knowing all this about the woman standing on the other side of the stone table did not explain why there was a villain in her quest cave in the first place.

CHAPTER SEVENTEEN

Despite Charlotte watching the events unfold before her with her own eyes, she couldn't bring herself to believe what she saw. It was true that challengers or champions regularly took part in quests and quest caves alike, but actual villains were never a part of anything.

This place makes no sense! We're back to this? None of the laws of magical worlds being followed? What does this mean?

Charlotte watched a foe they'd previously vanquished with nothing shy of total confusion. The Ice Queen's fingertips remained firmly planted on the stone table, her slow, steady breath misting in the frigid air as it puffed out from within the darkness of the cowl hiding her face. The chamber was silent, save for the occasional crack and snap of the frozen stone under her footsteps or her deadly, freezing touch.

The fairy godmother could hardly hear her own breathing, though it had slowed now that she had pinpointed the unwanted, uninvited presence in the quest chamber. Beside her, Cat stared at the hooded figure below, who was surrounded by concentric circles of frost and ice stretching farther away from the Ice Queen.

Charlotte slowly reached out to set a hand on Cat's back. Her fingers dug into his soft, fluffy, black fur, the warmth of his body reassuring her that she was still here, still conscious, and that all of this was real. It was the only way she could ground herself at that moment.

The low growl emanating from deep in the canine's chest was deep enough to be soundless, though Charlotte could feel it rumbling beneath her fingers with as much aggression and warning as if he had started barking and snarling at their foe from their hiding spot above.

Why is she here? It's one thing to somehow figure out a way to crash someone else's quest party, but something else entirely for her to have made it this far on her own. She looks like she knows exactly what she's doing, which doesn't make any sense if this is my quest. But she's up to something, all right. That much is obvious.

Charlotte felt the nearly uncontrollable urge to pounce right then and wring the queen's neck, but she recognized the need to know more first, or she could pounce to her death without even knowing it.

Whether or not Cat held some version of the same thought, he remained motionless beside her, non-responsive to the fairy godmother's fingers digging into his fur for reassurance.

After several more intensely long seconds, the Ice Queen finally moved. She removed one hand from the surface of the now frozen-over stone table. With a quick flick of her hand and a flash of brilliant silver-blue light, she conjured a small, quarter-sized, electric-blue stone resting in her open palm.

Charlotte's eyes widened when she recognized it immediately.

That's one of the ore stones from the mines and from the first tunnel we passed through when we first got here! she realized.

Another low growl came from the massive dog next to her. *Is that what I think it is? It feels the same.*

Charlotte nodded and whispered, "It is. I'm glad you saw it, too."

It was a stone very much like the one that almost wiped Alex entirely out of his own mind and put him under the closest thing the fairy godmother had seen to a sleeping curse since Aurora and Snow White.

"What is she doing with one of those?" she breathed.

Nothing good, I imagine.

Charlotte's anger nearly got the better of her, but she continued to knead into Cat's fur beside her. Before she could clench her fist and hurt him by yanking out a fistful of it, she took a slow, steady breath to calm herself.

The angry fairy godmother forced her hand open and let her palm lie flat on Cat's back, hoping it would make it harder to injure him if she were to forget she was there with her faithful companion.

A thousand thoughts ran through her mind. Everything from wondering if Alex and Sir Thomas were okay now that she knew a villain had been here the whole time to how the hell the Ice Queen got into a cave that Fate spelled to affect a specific group. It was why adventurers questing in groups had to enter caves together within seconds of one another. If Charlotte had entered and then Alex had followed thirty minutes later, he would have been inside alone.

The Ice Queen never entered the cave with them, so by all the laws that Charlotte knew that governed this sort of thing, the other woman should *not* have been able to be there. No matter how powerful she was. The only thing that Charlotte knew with absolute certainty was that whatever the Ice Queen was attempting down there, it wasn't good.

The Ice Queen seemed to stare at the glowing blue stone in her hand, though with her face hidden by a cowl, it was impossible to know for sure. Her breath misted into the frigid air from within the dark folds of the material. Another grating hiss and crackle filled the chamber, growing louder and more intense before echoing and dying again.

Charlotte couldn't tell where the sound was coming from until one final deafening crack filled the air, echoing through the entire chamber. A high-pitched squeal rose from below, and the glowing blue stone in the Ice Queen's palm dimmed, its light snuffed out like the life of a small, terrified creature. As the last speck of electric blue disappeared, the stone erupted.

Thousands of tiny, cold, splinter-sharp slivers of ruptured stone burst in all directions from the Ice Queen's open hand. The villain did not react, which made Charlotte think this was precisely what the woman had wanted.

It seemed the Ice Queen had perfected this act over time. Even as the shards of dull stone burst apart, she remained as still and sure as if handling feathers. She flicked her wrist and clenched her open palm into a tight, icy fist. Silvery white light illuminated every shard and splinter.

The Ice Queen had total control over the fragments. Each one froze in midair. Then, she slowly swept her fist over the table, and the shattered stone answered her call. The pieces, surrounded by the silvery white light of her frost magic, moved by her will alone. They settled into place along the surface of the stone altar, following the patterned gestures of her clenched fist.

Charlotte had never seen magic quite like this—neither the Ice Queen's delicate control over the element nor the ritual magic she used. The fairy godmother had experience with the queen's frost magic before, but battling and seeing fine, intricately detailed spells were two totally different things. If it weren't evil as hell, Charlotte would have been mesmerized by it. The ritual magic was attuned to movements and perhaps even words. Though, if the Ice Queen had been muttering an incantation, it must have been in the quietest hush of a whisper.

That psycho couldn't have come up with something like this on her own. That's not the Ice Queen's magic. She might be well-trained and powerful, but that isn't hers. Everything she has in her arsenal is all destruction and death, like launching spears of ice at her foes. This is something completely different. This is old magic.

The fairy godmother couldn't explain how she knew that to be true, only that there was no other explanation for the ritual magic the Ice Queen now used. It was a gut feeling Charlotte felt all the way past her gut and down to her bones. That magic did not belong to the Ice Queen, and that meant she'd stolen it from someone, either by force or because someone else was working with her and teaching her the spells.

Charlotte was more confident than she knew how to explain that the magic she currently watched the witch perform below should only be available to those who understood both how to control such forces and the implications of doing so.

Still, she could not look away from the mesmerizing display of the Ice Queen's ancient magical knowledge.

In seconds, a complicated, swirling shape had formed on the flat, surface of the stone slab table. Each shard of neutralized blue stone lay where the Ice Queen placed them with precision. Charlotte didn't recognize the symbol nor understand what was happening when the Ice Queen opened her fist, and the shards began to disappear.

No, not disappear. Diminish.

As Charlotte and Cat watched, the pieces grew smaller, almost as if they were sinking into the stone altar itself, being swallowed by the solid rock. It seemed impossible, but that was precisely what happened. Each sliver of ore disappeared beneath the surface as the icy, silvery blue light of the Ice Queen's magic flashed with finality. Then, the stone table somehow consumed all the pieces. To what end, Charlotte had no idea.

Even after all this time watching, nothing made any sense. Charlotte knew nothing more about the queen's plans or goals, and it made her leg move back and forth with anxiousness.

When the last shard became part of the table, the Ice Queen threw her arms wide, both hands extended, as if to reach across the entire cavern. The result of her next gesture was instantaneous.

A loud rumble rose through the chamber, coming from everywhere and nowhere at once. Charlotte realized it wasn't inside the chamber itself but all around it. A cold chill cut through her. Her jaw fell open, and her eyes widened as she recognized the sound. She recognized it because she'd encountered it more than anything else she had encountered since entering the quest cave with her companions.

It was the sound of an earthquake—another one ripping through the foundations of the earth, sending shuddering tremors through every bit of solid ground around them and moving outward. Because of the direction, it left the chamber completely untouched.

Anger burned in Charlotte's chest as she slowly took in this information and processed what it could mean.

She and her companions had experienced several of these warning rumbles and the increasingly violent earthquakes that followed. Charlotte couldn't even figure out how the Ice Queen had caused the quakes to begin with. The fairy godmother was even more confused about how the witch had *controlled* them once she'd started them.

How could she send them in a specific direction? The amount of power required to do such a thing seemed monumental to Charlotte.

There was only a slight vibration through the ledge at the top of the cliff leading into the cavern where the Ice Queen worked, but the ledge itself did not rock and pitch like the ground beneath them every other time an earthquake hit.

Everything within the ancient chamber Charlotte had believed was the end to her personal quest remained unaffected by the violence tearing through everywhere else within the cavern. And while she had no way to know for sure the earthquake was hitting the rest of the quest cave, everything in her said that was precisely the case.

Based on how much power Charlotte felt radiating from where the Ice Queen stood in the center of the chamber, Charlotte had a feeling this earthquake didn't only exist within the quest cave itself. Despite the fact that it existed in its own plane of existence, the fairy godmother believed these were powerful enough to reach into the human world.

These were likely the same earthquakes Charlotte and Alex had first felt in the woods outside Ginger Haus's hidden magical cottage. The same earthquakes the fairy godmother and her companions had been experiencing for weeks now in various locations. Even within Alex's apartment itself, though, the rest of the building had been unaffected, and none of the other residents had noticed anything.

They were the very same earthquakes that only Charlotte Weaver, Detective Alex Taylor, Sir Thomas, and Cat had felt because something specific about the four of them enabled them to feel the tremors—something that linked them to this place.

And now those earthquakes had followed Charlotte and her companions into the quest cave and this final chamber.

CHAPTER EIGHTEEN

That anger that twisted in her chest boiled over into full-on rage. They'd spent *weeks* trying to figure out what was happening. She'd even gone to Peter Pan over it. Though, had she not, she wouldn't have discovered the difficulties he faced there himself.

All that time. All that damage to Alex's apartment. It was her.

It's been her the whole time! She's the one causing the earthquakes with whatever that ritual is, using the stones. She's been down here all this time, endangering Cincinnati and all the other EverAfterans and disrupting magic. This is all her. How did she even accomplish such a thing?

Charlotte had even more questions now. How did the Ice Queen get the power to do this? What was the purpose? She wanted to go down there, grab the woman, and shake the hell out of her until she told her everything she wanted to know.

The trembling groan and rumble of the Ice Queen's newly conjured earthquake continued through the quest cave for what felt like ages. Though Charlotte could not possibly know for sure what was happening in any other part of the cave right now, she had a strong hunch that all the most critical areas of the quest cave were under direct assault from the Ice Queen's use of ancient dark magic.

The most critical areas within the quest cave involved the previous chamber she and Cat battled in, and she hoped like hell it wouldn't release The Demon. Surely, the Ice Queen wasn't *that* stupid. Even a villain like her would know a beast like that was uncontrollable. It would destroy her just as it would destroy everything else.

Another vital area was wherever Sir Thomas and Alex were now. And now that she understood what was happening, she realized the likelihood of them remaining where she'd left them was slim to none. There had been so many quakes, and so much damage had been sustained all over the cave that she felt confident the risk of death would have forced Sir Thomas to move the sleep-cursed Alex.

Guilt gripped her alongside the rage. *I just left them to fend for themselves in there.*

They didn't have any way to defend themselves against the earthquakes like she did. They couldn't have magically shielded themselves or healed themselves if they were injured. They didn't even have any means of escape unless the cave had opened a door for them too.

She worried she and Cat had left them in more danger than they could have possibly been in if they had gone with the fairy godmother and enchanted dog.

But that wasn't even an option. That stone archway stopped Alex from—

Charlotte sucked in a sharp breath when she realized how deeply rooted the Ice Queen's powers in this quest cave had been. Fortunately, the constant rumble of the next earthquake surging through the sacred magical site kept her gasp of surprise and horror from making too much noise. It didn't stop Charlotte from wanting to scream in fury at the Ice Queen for turning everything upside down.

That was her, too! It must have been!

There was no reason for Alex and Sir Thomas to stay behind unless that witch already had a hold on this place, and it was part of a bigger plan. If she'd enchanted the cavern to only let a fairy godmother through and no other type of EverAfterans or even humans, of course, she would have been forced to leave Sir Thomas and Alex behind.

She wanted to separate us, break us apart so we'd be easier to control, to defeat.

Gritting her teeth, Charlotte glanced over at Cat beside her. The canine's teeth bared in a silent snarl, and he did not once remove his sight from the Ice Queen, performing her ritual magic in front of the stone table.

"Have you realized what I have?" she questioned in a low voice.

Another low growl vibrated through him, the sound easily hidden by the tremors rocketing throughout the cave.

Yes. This entire thing, from the storm that pulled us through to this world until now, was all her doing. She's been controlling it all.

"Even more than that. All the quakes we felt back in Cincinnati—those were all her, too."

Cat's jowls peeled back further, revealing all his teeth as

drool gathered along his lower jawline before dripping slowly to the floor. She had a feeling he'd gladly relieve the witch of her head if he got the chance.

Charlotte was glad the Ice Queen didn't possess any spells to keep out cats from Earth, who had been enchanted into enormous dogs. *I was supposed to have been alone this whole time,* she realized. *If I had been, I never would have made it through the portal chamber.*

If it weren't for Cat, the fairy godmother likely would have lost her life on a faux quest, which was never meant to be and never would have happened if the witch hadn't weaseled her way in there to ruin everything.

How is this even possible? she wondered.

Now that all these things had made themselves apparent, Charlotte paid close attention to every detail of the chamber and the Ice Queen's work within it. She couldn't shake the feeling that there was something else she'd missed, something she should have discovered by now.

Presently, all she could focus on was the fact that the earthquake rattling the cave was lasting longer than any other so far. It was also potentially the most violent of them all to date. The earthquakes had started relatively small. Even though Charlotte and Alex had both been knocked off balance during the first one outside Ginger Haus's hidden cottage, it was still small in comparison to the ones she'd experienced in this cave.

Despite being unable to feel the brunt of the quake from her safe perch on the ledge—since it was clear that this chamber was immune—the fairy godmother worried for the rest of the cavern. If the Ice Queen didn't stop, she'd tear the whole damn thing apart from the inside and kill all of them in the process.

However, at this point, Charlotte believed that might have been her plan.

The fairy godmother waited impatiently for the violent rumbling within the rest of the quest cave to cease. Her worry for Alex and Sir Thomas grew to new heights. They were powerless against this. If she and Cat didn't find a way to get down there and stop the witch, she feared the other half of their party would be lost for good.

Please let Alex and Sir Thomas be alive. Please let them be safe from this.

Despite the fairy godmother's penchant for clinging to positivity and hope, Charlotte found herself now understanding more than ever before what it felt like to watch hope dwindle right before your eyes. Every second longer that the terrible trembling within the cave persisted was another bit of hope the fairy godmother felt die.

Seeing the Ice Queen down there in what Charlotte had believed was her personal quest cave had shaken her belief in many things. After all, a quest cave was meant to test an adventurer's worthiness, resolve, and readiness for battles. They weren't supposed to be controlled by power-hungry lunatics and wholly endanger the adventurers with life-threatening circumstances.

But the Ice Queen was here, and because of that, everything about this place had thrown the fairy godmother for a loop.

The detective being rendered unconscious almost immediately, the stone archway blocking Alex's passage, the endless corridors she had traversed with Cat, the countless creatures within the portal chamber, and the fact that this quest cave didn't follow *any* of the laws or rules she'd learned in the Guild.

The earthquakes were all connected as well. Even the glowing blue ore Charlotte, Sir Thomas, and Cat had first found beneath Cincinnati's abandoned subway tunnels in the mines the humans of this world clearly had no idea existed. These were all connected. Everything Charlotte and her companions had experienced with them had all come about at the direction of the Ice Queen.

It all made so much more sense now. It even explained how a quest cave like this could unleash something like The Demon upon its adventurers. In reality, that had not been the doing of this sacred, sentient, magical place but instead a result of the Ice Queen's presence here.

At last, Charlotte understood that this cave was every-thing she believed it to be: an enchanted place in a realm that existed between realms. It was meant to challenge heroes just as the ones she'd seen and learned about in others' stories.

But this particular quest cave never called out to her to test her as a hero on its own accord. Instead, the Ice Queen had lured and trapped Charlotte and her group inside in hopes of defeating them.

However, because of that, Charlotte was being tested anyway. Her goal wasn't to prove herself to the cave. Her goal now was to *save* the cave before the Ice Queen abso-lutely destroyed it. And because the fairy godmother and her friends were trapped there, saving the cave meant saving those she loved most and saving herself.

I can't fail, she thought.

How that vile woman had found this sacred quest cave in the first place, or how long she'd been here, was anyone's guess. What mattered was that the Ice Queen had found a way to affect Charlotte, her companions, and every step they had taken since their first run-in with Prince Repel's old ally after she had attacked Alex's apartment and rendered it unlivable for a few weeks.

According to Pan, none of the other EverAfterans had felt these earthquakes, which must also have been by design. However, even if they hadn't felt them physically, that hadn't stopped the quakes from affecting the Ever-Afterans in other ways.

The chaos, inexplicable animosity, and violence among the EverAfteran denizens of Peter Pan's sanctuary at the docks now made perfect sense, too. Charlotte made a mental note to go to the docks when she returned to Cincinnati—and without a doubt, the fairy godmother knew that she *would* return—to tell Peter Pan what had happened and why his people had suffered as they had.

None of them would have discovered who was truly behind these vile changes if Charlotte and her companions had not entered the quest cave. The same could be said if she and Cat had not survived the rotating portal chamber, which she was now certain had been modified by the Ice Queen to kill them before they could make it this far.

The only question that remained for her was, what does the ore have to do with anything? It was obvious the witch knew how to use its power, but Charlotte couldn't figure out what the ore was *supposed* to be used for or even *how* to use it.

How else was the ore involved, and how had the Ice

Queen found herself with such vast knowledge of how to use it?

The rumbling of the Ice Queen's most recent earthquake continued. Despite being beyond the worst of the quake's effects, even the chamber now trembled slightly under the growling, rumbling power that was likely ripping the quest cave apart from the inside out.

Small pebbles, stones, and sheaves of dust toppled down from the chamber's ceiling, clicking and clacking on the stone ledge in front of the fairy godmother and her canine companion. If this got any worse, Charlotte realized she might have to bubble them. If she did, they'd have to move back far enough that the witch couldn't see or sense the fairy godmother's magic, which would keep Charlotte from seeing anything else the queen was doing below.

Then, and not a moment too soon, the earthquake finally died into a low growl and a sputtering shiver before halting completely. No more rumbling, violent cracking, or tearing through the earth in this enchanted place that should have been immune to such things.

Charlotte's lips curled into a silent snarl as she watched the villainous woman prepare to enact the next part of her ritual. Whatever it was, she had a feeling it would somehow be worse. After all, situations like this only continued to get worse until someone stopped the person responsible. The fairy godmother was perfectly happy to be that person, but without knowing exactly what was happening, she had no idea how to stop it or reverse what the witch had done.

She and Alex had seen firsthand what happened when they dove blindly to thwart a threat they assumed they knew all about, only to realize they had misread the situation. Admittedly, there was little to misread in this specific situation.

The Ice Queen had somehow gained an advantage over the fairy godmother and all the EverAfterans who had been banished to Cincinnati. She had no doubt there would be no point when she realized the Ice Queen was a misunderstood woman who wanted to save people. This was cut and dried.

However, if Charlotte had any hope of fixing everything the witch had destroyed, the fairy godmother would need to exercise patience and only interfere when the time was right or if there was no other choice. Otherwise, she risked being unable to undo the damage the Ice Queen had caused.

"We have to wait for her to show her hand, and then we can jump in. Then, we can bring the fight to her and ensure whatever else she has planned never comes to fruition. I just have to know what that is first."

Agreed, Cat offered with a low chuff.

Fortunately, Charlotte didn't have to wait long for the Ice Queen to do just that.

Once the last of the tremors died down, the Ice Queen prepared for whatever the next phase of her plan was. She lifted both hands to grab the edge of her cowl that shrouded her face in darkness and let it fall behind her neck.

The woman's face was exactly as Charlotte remembered it: pale skin like ice, glittering, frosty blue eyes, delicately chiseled features, from her high cheekbones to the rounded jut of her chin and the crisp line of her small, hard nose. Frost-white hair spilled from her head, disappearing beneath her dark cloak.

A surge of furious determination rose in the fairy godmother, but Charlotte forced herself to remain still and silent. Whatever the Ice Queen was doing, it clearly wasn't over yet.

Nearly all of Charlotte Weaver's willpower and training shattered when the Ice Queen reached into the folds of her cloak and produced a large, ancient tome. Chills raced through the fairy godmother that had nothing to do with the draft wafting up from the floor of the chamber.

The volume was agonizingly familiar even before the frosty witch held it aloft with her cold, pale fingers and lowered it reverently onto the gleaming stone slab where she'd performed all her ritual magic.

Charlotte recognized that book, from the size and color of the cover to the shade of the aged tan pages along the edges. It was a book she'd know anywhere because she owned one just like it.

Only hers remained scattered throughout Cincinnati and this very cave.

CHAPTER NINETEEN

Charlotte stared in wide-eyed shock. She felt like she couldn't breathe. Her chest ached with the need to gasp, and her heart now galloped in her chest.

No. How in the world did she—

Charlotte couldn't even finish the thought. The mere act of acknowledging that such a thing was possible, that such a thing had happened, ripped her heart out. But there was the proof lying on that stone table right in front of her in the chamber below.

The large, powerful tome the Ice Queen had produced from some hidden pocket within her thick, dark cloak was undoubtedly a fairy godmother's handbook. It looked exactly like Charlotte's had before her accidental banishment to Cincinnati, which had ripped apart her own handbook page by page.

There was only one other fairy godmother this possibly could have belonged to—one of Charlotte's sisters, who had perished in her last battle but somehow left her handbook behind and intact.

This one belonged to the fairy godmother, Belinda. It was the very same handbook Prince Repel had gotten his grimy little hands on, allowing him to work powerful and complicated magic from the nearly magic-less human world and the city of Cincinnati, Ohio.

How did the Ice Queen get it?

Despite how seeing the handbook in the Ice Queen's hands made her feel, she realized how it got there hardly mattered now. The terrible truth was that the Ice Queen had Belinda's handbook, which explained everything. Charlotte watched as the other woman worked the incredibly powerful magic within the ancient pages with her own hands.

The ever-present rage in Charlotte's chest bloomed tenfold when she thought about everything they'd been through, all for her to have to sit there and watch the witch below use something that belonged to someone important to the fairy godmother. Someone who had died in battle, which made her an honorable woman.

The Ice Queen had no business even *looking* at Belinda's handbook, let alone using it!

Even though she had not yet fully observed what the Ice Queen intended to do with Belinda's spell book, Charlotte found her boiling rage and indignation pushing her to the point when sitting and waiting for the right time would no longer be possible. Her clenched fists trembled as she pressed them against the floor where she lay at the edge of the ledge, marking the sharp drop into the chamber.

Charlotte's breath quickened in ragged gasps as she struggled to hold her tongue and remain silent, still trying to avoid giving away her position. Those attempts nearly failed as the Ice Queen leaned over the stone slab with a dark, victorious sneer.

When the villain reached out with a bony hand to attempt to open the spell book and siphon more of its power—perhaps even to enact some of the dangerous and sacred spells only fairy godmothers were qualified to cast —Charlotte's control snapped entirely, and she moved back.

She couldn't stand to hide in silence one second longer, forced to watch the Ice Queen debase the only thing that still existed of her sister fairy godmother, Belinda.

Her sense of honor and duty filled her with the undeniable need to do something, and she needed to do it now.

Before the Ice Queen's frozen touch could settle onto the cover of Belinda's handbook, Charlotte leaped to her feet and walked to the ledge.

"Don't you dare touch that!" she shouted, her voice echoing violently around the chamber.

Now that Charlotte was on her feet, Cat had no qualms about climbing to his as well. Suddenly, the sound of his deep, vicious growl echoed around the chamber, and the fairy godmother knew he'd been holding it in.

Is that what I think it is?

"Yes," she answered, her voice filled with unchecked hatred. "It belonged to my dead sister godmother, Belinda."

Cat lowered his head, his jowls pulling back further. *Then we'll rip her apart if we have to and get it back.*

Charlotte was surprised momentarily by the tone of his mental voice and also by the viciousness of his words, but it warmed her somehow.

She quickly realized, however, that his quickness to

violence shouldn't have been shocking. After all, he was initially a cat. Statistically, the common house cat was the deadliest among all the Earth cats, including lions, tigers, and jaguars, because they hunted for fun and killed indiscriminately with a high success rate. Larger species of cats only hunted for food and were rarely successful, resulting in some of the species only eating once a week or so.

She never would have known that if Alex hadn't told Sir Thomas that fact as a way to make him feel better after the detective had insulted the talking cat.

Upon hearing Charlotte's voice and Cat's angry growl, the Ice Queen froze, retracting her hand as she searched for the source of the shout. At first, she looked confused and slightly worried about hearing such a furious call without seeing its origin. But then, she looked up and found what she'd been searching for.

Her icy blue eyes widened, and then a slow, self-satisfied snarl curled her lips. "Fairy Godmother, what a surprise. You're alive." Her eyes wandered over, and a single brow lifted. "Oh, and look... You figured out how to bring a friend. How nice of you to drop in."

"I'm sure our survival pisses you off," Charlotte snapped back. "Especially after all the trouble you've gone through to stop me from reaching this chamber. But now I'm here, and whatever you're planning is finished. If you continue, I can assure you that all the rage I feel after everything you've put us through will fuel me, and you won't like what comes for you."

The Ice Queen let out a sharp bark of bitter laughter and shook her head. "Oh, you try so hard, don't you?"

Her hand reached for the book again, and Charlotte

kicked a softball-sized rock off the ledge at the witch. It narrowly missed the other woman, hitting the stone table and breaking into several pieces before landing on the floor and scattering. The Ice Queen jumped back.

The witch laughed again, the sound mocking and sour as she fluttered her fingers in the fairy godmother's direction. "Someone's gotten themselves all riled up now, haven't they?"

"Don't you dare touch that handbook," Charlotte shouted, pointing her wand at the Ice Queen. Only now did she realize her hand no longer shook.

Once again, the witch reached slowly toward the cover of Belinda's handbook, her pale skeletal fingers elongating in the low light of the chamber. "Oh... You mean *this* handbook?"

"Celeste!" Charlotte roared. "That does not belong to you!" The unquestionable authority in Charlotte's voice would have startled her if she hadn't been so focused on glaring at the cold-hearted sorceress across the table.

The force of her shout brought several small pebbles tumbling free from the chamber wall. She had already brandished her wand at the Ice Queen, which was sure to escalate matters, but she couldn't help it.

For the first time in a very long time, Charlotte Weaver was incapable of separating her emotions from her work, even in such a tense situation. She didn't lie. Emotion fueled her magic. Usually, that emotion was an overwhelming sense of determination.

Now, it was pure, undeniable hatred, and whatever she did would no doubt be powerful and dangerous.

The Ice Queen scowled at the unexpected use of her

given name. Though it wouldn't deter her, she did not appreciate the fairy godmother's boldness. "You don't know a thing about me, Fairy Godmother, but you will. You will learn *exactly* what I'm capable of. And how hopeless it is to try to stop me."

Charlotte had never been one to believe people started off as bad. She'd always had the belief that villains weren't born. They were created. And if that were true, that meant whatever Celeste had been through in her lifetime was terrible enough to send her down a path that made her hate everything good in the world.

In *all* worlds.

But that didn't give her license to *hurt* those who were good.

"You're right. I don't know a damn thing about you. I know you're like every other villain out there. Hurt. Betrayed. Forsaken. Something in your lifetime broke your heart *so* badly that you cut everything and everyone else in the world off to the point your capability to love died."

When Charlotte paused to take a breath, Celeste spoke. "Something like that."

The fairy godmother nodded. "Yeah, I figured as much. And while my soul aches for the innocent part of you that died the day someone chose to break your spirit, I'm also enraged at your ability to take your pain and suffering out on others. On those who had nothing to do with what happened to you. Nothing you've been through gives you the right to hurt others, Celeste. Whatever this is? It's done. Leave my sister's book. Leave this place. Don't make me do this. Don't make me fight you."

The Ice Queen scoffed. "Beautiful speech. Spoken like a

woman who has never known true tragedy." Charlotte was about to respond when Celeste spoke again, sending angry chills down the fairy godmother's spine. "But you will. I've been watching you, you know. You seem quite smitten with that human I placed the sleep curse on." She smiled. "He's cute. I see why you like him, but I'm more curious to see what happens when you lose him. If you still hold on to that self-righteous, good-always-triumphs-over-evil bull-shit view of the world that you seem to take so seriously. My guess is a resounding *no.*"

Charlotte's nostrils flared when she mentioned Alex. The witch knew her soft spot, but Charlotte had yet to find Celeste's.

"You've done more than enough. Stop now. Leave this realm and leave that spell book!" Charlotte shouted.

The Ice Queen's hand inched closer to the large, worn, leather-bound tome that had once been the source of another fairy godmother's power and magical knowledge. "Are you sure?" She leered at Charlotte and reached further toward the handbook. "Oh, I see… You think this belongs to one of your own, don't you? Another fairy godmother, right? Which one was she again? Ah, yes. The *dead one.*"

Charlotte gritted her teeth, the fury building inside her momentarily paralyzing her.

The Ice Queen took that as an invitation to keep talking. "It might have belonged to that pitiful excuse for a fairy godmother at one point, sure. But that was a long time ago, wasn't it? She's been dead a *long* time, sweetheart." When Charlotte growled and clenched her fists, Celeste laughed before continuing. "Since then, *several* other hands have touched this book. Not just mine. I recovered this from what was left of Repel once you and your little friends disposed of him. That was a poor choice on your part, Fairy Godmother, because something else was unleashed the day Prince Repel was vanquished. And how convenient that no one saw it coming."

"What, you?" Charlotte scoffed and then laughed heartily, briefly throwing her head back. "You think you're so much worse?"

The Ice Queen's sneer intensified. "It is so like you and all your kind to think in such small, insignificant terms, Fairy Godmother. None of you have the mind for vengeance. None of you possess the darkness required to think like we do and figure us out before we strike because you couldn't fathom going to the lengths we do. But that's all about to change. I'm almost finished here, and once I am, no fairy godmother in EverAfter, this world, or any other, will wield the same power you once did. No one will look to you to save them. No one will call your name in their darkest hour. Because after this, everyone will know exactly how useless and weak your Guild truly is. There's nothing you can do to stop it."

The sorceress's hand lashed out toward the cover of Belinda's handbook again, but Charlotte had recovered her wits and was faster than her foe expected.

"No!" she bellowed, flicking her wand toward the Ice Queen and the stone table with a violent twitch of her wrist.

The blazing golden light from Charlotte's wand was unexpected, even to her. There was no specific directive, no words to channel her spell as it had been in EverAfter, where magic behaved as it should under her command.

Celeste was wrong. Charlotte wasn't like the godmothers she knew. Hell, she wasn't even like she was before finding herself banished to Cincinnati. Charlotte had a mind of her own, and it was *quite* capable of feeling blind rage and a thirst for vengeance. And still, even with all that, the godmother's crystal-clear intention was to stop the Ice Queen before she could make another move and drastically affect all worlds and all the beings who called those worlds home.

Charlotte's spell shot straight down over the ledge into the ancient room. With a strobing flicker, the magic struck the stone table directly in front of the Ice Queen. A crackling ripple of power surged into the sorceress's hand and the late Belinda's handbook simultaneously.

The Ice Queen hissed at the jarring pain of the fairy godmother's warning shot and instantly retracted her hand. The handbook skittered across the wide, surface of the stone table and out of her reach.

With a snarl, the Ice Queen glared up at the raised platform where the fairy godmother stood with her wand at the ready, and a growling, teeth-baring Cat crouched at her side.

"It's over," Charlotte snapped, taking one more step toward the edge. With the level of anger she had fueling her, she was no longer worried about the strength of her wings *or* her magic. "The sooner you accept that, the sooner I can decide what to do with you."

"It will never be over, Fairy Godmother," the Ice Queen hissed. "Not until all of you pay for what you've done. Only after I have stood over the ashes of both these worlds to spit on all your graves will I listen to your dying words. Maybe you can find me then, hmm?"

The Ice Queen thrust her hand across the stone table to reach for Belinda's handbook again. An icy blue light welled in her palm, flickering around the handbook's leather-bound cover.

And that was when Charlotte lost all thought of what a decorated, trained fairy godmother would do in a situation like this. She lost control of herself entirely. Everything after that was the strength of magic in this place responding to the strength of what Charlotte Weaver had been fighting so hard to accomplish.

A scream of fury and grief tore from her throat—grief over the loss of Belinda, for the loss of her own handbook that meant so much to her, for all the things she and her companions could have accomplished if the Ice Queen hadn't constantly thwarted them.

Then there was the grief she felt at having been violently ripped from her home world and thrown into Cincinnati, a place she didn't know, surrounded by humans who didn't believe she was who and what she always had been. And finally, grief for all those harmed by the Fairy Godmothers' Guild and their grossly misused banishment portal, and the debilitating effects banishment had on everyone, villains and innocent EverAfterans alike.

So, Charlotte wasn't thinking at all when she cast her next spell and screamed down into the chamber with everything she was worth.

A brilliant golden light burst from the tip of her wand, cracking violently against the stone table. Fireworks of every color exploded across the table's surface before shooting out in all directions, including straight at the Ice Queen.

The magic's force threw the sorceress backward, her arms flailing and her dark cloak whipping out as she sailed through the air. The second she landed on the cold stone floor with a muffled thump and a startled grunt of pain, Charlotte's spell began to take root within the chamber, producing unexpected results.

The ledge on which she and Cat stood shuddered, then lurched forward. It didn't break away from the chamber wall but elongated, growing outward with more stone. It grew until it turned at a sharp downward angle, elongated further, then flattened out again. Over and over, the stone ledge repeated this transformation, jutting outward and rippling down until the intended shape became clear.

They're stairs. How the hell did I do that?

Instead of wasting time overthinking it, she placed her trust in her magic and its capabilities to accomplish the inconceivable. Now, instead of a seventy-foot drop, Charlotte had one hell of a runway, and run she did.

She and Cat ran as fast as they could down the stone stairs to reach the bottom before the Ice Queen could recover. The fairy godmother kept her wand raised and aimed directly at Celeste's chest. The stairs hadn't yet fully built themselves down to the chamber floor, but they kept pace with her and Cat, and that's all she needed.

As the stairs continued to form, the new structure twisted on itself repeatedly, circling the room as it made its way to the bottom. *Not fast enough!* she thought to herself.

"Cat, keep running. Don't stop. I can't wait any longer," she said.

Cat barked behind her. *Go! I'll be at the bottom soon.*

The fairy godmother leaped into the air when the steps were halfway down into the chamber. Her wings furiously beat as they carried her directly toward her adversary. The closer she got to the Ice Queen, the angrier Charlotte became. Her wings worked faster than she remembered, and in no time, she landed just three yards from where the Ice Queen was now attempting to pick herself up.

All of it had happened in seconds, and the sorceress had not had enough time to realize what Charlotte was doing, let alone prepare to meet her head-on, but head-on, they did meet.

The Ice Queen had barely managed to prop herself up on one knee, grimacing from the pain of Charlotte throwing her back from the table and her prized fairy godmother's handbook. Not wanting to give the other woman a chance to recover, Charlotte let loose a brilliant flash of magic from her wand, striking the Ice Queen's hip.

With a shriek of rage, Celeste went flying again. This time, however, she did not go nearly as far as the first blast sent her, and she landed hard on her side. The distraction gave Charlotte plenty of time to leap and flutter forward. Her wings beat urgently before her feet touched down between her adversary and the altar.

Brandishing her wand, Charlotte pointed its powerful tip at the sorceress who had meddled in her affairs for far too long. The godmother lifted her chin defiantly, staring down the witch. She was ready to take the Ice Queen out if necessary. After everything the other woman had done to Charlotte and her friends—including trying to separate and kill them—the fairy godmother had no issue doing whatever needed to be done in defense of the ones she loved.

"If you don't end whatever the hell this is, I promise things won't end well for you," Charlotte warned, her voice dropping low. "And just so you know... While I'm *fully* ready to end you if you force my hand—because I *am* capable of vengeance and rage—I really don't want to watch anyone else get hurt. Even after all you've done. The choice is yours. We can walk away from this fight right now, provided we come to an agreement with a few magically binding provisions. The other option is that I find something *very* unpleasant for you. Maybe the threat of a few minutes in with The Demon will sway you in the right direction? What do you think?"

The fairy godmother knew with absolute confidence that the cave itself had been the one to save her and Cat from The Demon. The cave had been the one to manifest the door that freed them. Celeste wouldn't have done such a thing. She'd summoned it to kill Charlotte.

Because the cave was sentient and meant to change depending on what an individual quest required for each individual hero, the cave knew its only chance of survival would die with Charlotte. The ancient, enchanted site was able to break away from Celeste's control long enough to free her and Cat, and she wouldn't betray that act of faith now.

Charlotte lifted her chin, holding her ground and eyeing the Ice Queen's reaction over the bridge of her nose, her wand still trained on the sorceress. In the background, the chamber filled with the rumbling sounds of the stone staircase unfolding from the ledge above. Cat's mad, ceaseless barking echoed as he ran down the spiraling stairs, his claws clacking across each step.

Somehow, Charlotte drowned it all out to focus on the witch's response.

For a moment, it seemed the other woman was ready to admit defeat, lacking better options against what might have been the only fairy godmother in history to offer a villain a second chance before the worst of the fighting had even begun.

She wouldn't have made the other woman that offer before the portal took her to Cincinnati. However, if the Fairy Godmothers' Guild was responsible for manufacturing villains and wrongfully sentencing their own people to a world that didn't belong to them, someone needed to break that cycle.

It seems that someone's me, seeing as I'm the only fairy godmother who knows about the conspiracy and is willing to change it.

The Ice Queen stared at the tip of Charlotte's wand aimed at her face as she breathed heavily on the floor. Her chest heaved, and her glittering blue eyes flickered toward Charlotte's face and then behind her at something else in the chamber.

Her mouth curled into a sneer. "Is that it? You think you can just hold me at wand-point and threaten me like that?"

"This isn't a threat," Charlotte said evenly with a shake of her head. "It's an ultimatum. Stop this now, and we can still work something out that's beneficial for both of us. I promise you won't get a better deal from any other fairy godmother. In fact, I would go so far as to say I'm the *only* godmother who would offer you this, and it's because of the things I've learned while in the human world."

The Ice Queen barked out a sharp laugh.

"Or you can keep going," Charlotte continued. "You can keep trying to tear everything down around you. If you're using Belinda's handbook, it can't be good. I might not know exactly what you're trying to do, but if it has to do with the Guild, I have a feeling I can give a pretty accurate guess as to your reasons. What I do know is that this won't end well for you if you keep challenging me and standing in my way. You said I don't know you. Well, you don't know me either, or I think we might be on neutral ground if we tried, even if we didn't like each other. Personally, I'd like to stop seeing painful, unhappy endings when a happy ending for everyone still exists. I'm willing to help you find it."

Cat finally reached the bottom of the staircase, leaping the last few feet to land beside Charlotte. His claws skidded to a halt on the stone, his attention on the Ice Queen as he crouched low, baring his teeth and letting out a long, low growl.

That took a little longer than expected.

Charlotte quickly eyed her companion and gave an acknowledging nod before returning her attention to the Ice Queen. They were all here on the same level, and Charlotte had managed to thwart the sorceress's attempts to use Belinda's handbook for the worst types of magic imaginable.

The immediate threat was over. With a wand at her fingertips, how much of a threat could the other woman be? Especially when it looked like the Ice Queen was starting to listen to what Charlotte had to say.

A small, genuine smile flickered across Charlotte's lips as she glanced at Cat crouching by her side. She then turned back to the Ice Queen and shrugged. "He'll never actually say it out loud, but my four-legged friend here also believes in second chances, which is exactly what you could have if you let me help you. To be honest, I'm pretty sure we could help each other with quite a lot. I want to know your story, and I want to tell you *why* I want to know, but I need to know I can trust you. That you won't hurt any other innocents. So, what do you say?"

The Ice Queen glanced between Charlotte and Cat, her ice-blue eyes wide and as she mulled over her options.

Charlotte felt she'd handled the situation well. If Celeste were as reasonable as Charlotte hoped, villain or not, she had a feeling they would come to a mutually beneficial agreement in the next few minutes. After all, if the witch was after the Guild for hurting her to the point of becoming a villain, then Charlotte wanted to do everything in her power to right that wrong and help stop the Guild from doing it to anyone else.

That was something the fairy godmother had never expected to anticipate during any assignment: the desire to save a villain and work alongside them for true justice instead of delivering punishment. But far too much had changed in the last few months.

There was no going back now.

Not even if she wanted to.

CHAPTER TWENTY

Sir Thomas had fully believed that once he and the unconscious Detective Alex Taylor narrowly escaped the last cavern, the bulk of the immediate danger was over. It wasn't every day that one avoided being pulverized by falling chunks of stone from a magically induced earthquake.

Despite spending most of their questing time effectively alone and unable to do much, Detective Taylor's unconscious company had provided some balm to Sir Thomas' loneliness.

The talking cat had a hunch that he and Charlotte were correct in assuming that the interference she'd experienced with her magic in Cincinnati was due to the earthquakes. Though they didn't know their origin back then or how to stop them, he couldn't deny the coincidence was far too big to ignore. And if they really had originated here, once they discovered how to stop them, he held hope that the magical interference would cease.

Then, things could return to normal, or as relatively normal as Sir Thomas and his party had come to accept over the last several months.

The last earthquake had caused the enormous chamber he and his human companion had narrowly escaped minutes before to cave in. At least, Sir Thomas thought it had only been minutes. The trouble was, in a place like this, time stopped working the way it was supposed to. Minutes felt like hours, and then hours somehow felt like minutes sometimes. There was no rhyme or reason to it.

For all he knew, he could have been leading his unconscious friend through the slightly illuminated tunnel for endless hours by now. Either way, he was sure that Lady Charlotte's protective magic made their escape and their trek down this new corridor much easier. The magic made Detective Taylor particularly light and easy to maneuver, even for a bipedal cat standing little more than three feet tall on his hind legs.

Despite the protective spell shrouding Alex, Sir Thomas took great care not to bump the detective into the walls. He had already experienced plenty of that in the last cavern while trying to avoid falling rocks and make their escape before becoming a permanent fixture in the quest cave.

Stepping into a place like this hardly makes us quest adventurers like I always thought it did. That moniker is reserved for brave souls who aren't relegated to the role of unconscious human babysitter.

Sir Thomas had plenty to be frustrated about. When they were transported together as a group from the woods outside Ginger's suburban home to the in-between realm in which the quest cave resided, that meant this quest was offered to all four members as a team.

The swashbuckling cat had been the first to swear his oath to Lady Charlotte, promising to fight at her side, protect her, follow her orders, and remain with her through the entirety of the quest, whether it led to victory or a bitter end.

Yet Lady Charlotte had chosen him to stay behind with the unconscious Detective Taylor because someone needed to watch the man to ensure no harm came to him. Even though he'd accepted his fate, Sir Thomas was still rankled at the thought of how much more he could have accomplished had he been allowed to continue with Lady Charlotte instead of remaining in the cavern with Detective Taylor.

Cat somehow convinced the fairy godmother in record time that Sir Thomas was perfect for babysitting duties, but as usual, he was right. This made him angry at the time, and that anger grew for quite some time, but it diminished once he stopped and thought about the logistics. The decision made sense.

While a formidable opponent, Cat would have needed to be better equipped to protect Alex from falling boulders and razor-sharp sheets of rock. And while Lady Charlotte's protective magic did much to keep Alex safe, Sir Thomas doubted even that spell would have saved Alex from being flattened between falling boulders and the cavern floor, which, to his credit, was all Sir Thomas' doing.

Most importantly, had Cat been the one to stay behind and watch the detective, he would have been incapable of communing with the fairy godmother so they could find their way to one another or as close to it as they were likely to get after the most recent earthquake.

Though he hesitated to admit it, Sir Thomas was fully aware that he and Alex probably would not have made it out of that chamber had Lady Charlotte's calls not reached his ears at the exact moment they were needed. She'd led him to the second stone archway as a viable escape route, which had appeared within the chamber wall mere seconds after one of the previous earthquakes had finished breaking through the earth and the underground chamber and maybe even the entirety of the quest cave itself.

Cat is an excellent companion, but he might have been overwhelmed by all the noise and chaos and unable to make it through that second archway while also pulling Detective Taylor along with him.

It was surprisingly tricky to gauge how long it had been since Sir Thomas last heard Lady Charlotte calling through the labyrinth of passageways. After the cavern's collapse, the talking cat had been momentarily stunned, but Lady Charlotte had coaxed him onward, promising that they would reunite their party and continue their quest together.

It seemed odd at first that Sir Thomas could hear the fairy godmother so clearly without her being right there ahead of him, but it *was* an enchanted cave. Not to mention, she had her magic back. Who was to say she didn't use magic to carry her words?

When he asked about that very thing, she explained that the enchanted walls of the quest cave allowed sound to travel great distances. This seemed perfectly rational to him, and he was heartened by the prospect of reuniting with the others whenever he heard Cat's happy bark in the distance.

The oddity of not understanding Cat's barks soon ran its course. Sir Thomas assumed it was due to the distance since his ability to understand the enchanted dog's words relied on close physical proximity. It was no stranger than being unable to discern a whisper from the opposite end of the cave.

So, Sir Thomas continued onward, pushing Detective Taylor's levitating body with his paws on the man's shoulders.

He thoroughly expected to hear Lady Charlotte's voice calling toward him from down the corridor at any moment. It felt like it had been quite some time since they last spoke, and Lady Charlotte was the type to check in frequently with her companions in case issues arose that required immediate discussion and new plans.

After continuing for what he believed was another fifteen minutes, Sir Thomas decided to initiate another conversation himself.

"Lady Charlotte?" he called through the dimly lit passage. "My lady, are you there? Can you still hear me?"

He almost stopped pushing the floating detective to listen for any sounds from up ahead. Then he remembered that any time spent waiting and searching without moving forward was time wasted, and that was the last thing any of them wanted: more wasted time. The earthquakes had steadily increased in frequency, duration, and intensity with every new tremor.

So, the sooner Sir Thomas and Detective Taylor

reunited with the rest of their party, the better. They would be much safer together, and that was exactly what Sir Thomas intended to prioritize.

He was momentarily taken by surprise when Lady Charlotte's voice rose through the very walls around him mere minutes later. Her voice seemed to come from everywhere at once, including the edges of the corridor, the spaces beyond, and from up ahead in the semi-darkness that even his keen feline vision could not see through.

"Sir Thomas? Sir Thomas, can you hear me?"

He stopped in his tracks, waiting for her voice to rise again before he spun left, then right, and finally, all the way around to look behind him, all the while keeping one paw on Detective Taylor's shoulder.

"I can hear you just fine, my lady," he called back. "It's difficult to tell where you are, though."

"Don't worry about that right now," she said. "We'll find each other soon. I'm just relieved to know that you're both safe and still on your way through the tunnels. Are you both okay? The last few quakes have been powerful."

He almost scoffed but held himself in check out of respect for the fairy godmother, whom he very much considered a friend. "We're moving through the tunnels, my lady. It's quite difficult to discern exactly how far we've come or how long it has taken us to get to this point. Are you and Cat having any better luck?"

"Cat and I are fine. We can only go as far as we are now, however. You'll have to travel the rest of the way to us. Hurry if you can because I would rather not force any of us to remain here longer than necessary."

Under different circumstances, the hint of disappointment and sadness in the fairy godmother's voice, though well-masked, would have made Sir Thomas desperate to reassure her. But these circumstances were far from ordinary, and there was little he could do but continue walking down the darkened corridor, lit mainly by the silvery glow surrounding Detective Taylor ahead of him.

Only when they finally found Lady Charlotte and Cat could he assess how to ease her doubts and fears. For now, he had to focus on getting through this damnable tunnel.

"We're on our way, my lady," he said with a curt nod despite knowing she couldn't see it. "Detective Taylor and I should find you before you know it. You have my word."

"And I have every faith in your ability to keep it, Sir Thomas. We'll see each other soon."

Unlike previous conversations with Lady Charlotte, the end of this one was disconcerting. As soon as the godmother finished her response, a cold draft hurtled down the corridor as if the tunnel led to a deserted tundra and someone had opened the door to let in the stinging air.

Despite his belief in logic and reason, Sir Thomas couldn't shake the feeling that the end of his conversation with Lady Charlotte and the cold draft were somehow related.

Don't be ridiculous. Lady Charlotte doesn't control the weather. We can continue in the cold just as well as we could in the previous temperature within the tunnels.

He decided it was best not to dwell on the what-ifs.

"Don't worry, Detective. I'll continue to carry out my duties to both you and Lady Charlotte to the best of my honed, though currently limited, capabilities. I'm confident we'll find them soon."

With that, he continued down the corridor, pushing Alex along by his shoulders and humming a wordless tune. The temperature dropped more as they traveled toward their hopeful rendezvous point with Lady Charlotte and Cat, but Sir Thomas chalked it up to the likelihood that they were now farther below the surface.

CHAPTER TWENTY-ONE

Charlotte stood over the Ice Queen, who still hadn't managed to pick herself up from the cold stone floor of the ancient chamber. The sorceress glowered at the fairy godmother with wide eyes and remained far too silent for Charlotte's liking.

She's thinking about it, weighing the pros and cons, and trying to make the best decision.

The fairy godmother wanted to believe that the Ice Queen was truly considering her proposition of working together, of coming to some sort of agreement that could enable them both to walk away with something positive.

A compromise.

That simple word and the seemingly simple concept behind it had been a keystone pillar of all the things fairy godmothers were trained to keep in mind upon entering the Guild. After everything Charlotte had learned about the Fairy Godmothers' Guild, she believed that compromise was exactly the tool she needed to succeed in her current endeavors.

Especially when she was trying to help—and maybe even save—this violent, furious, cold-hearted, vengeful witch seeking to wreak havoc on two worlds as well as this in-between realm. According to everything Charlotte knew, and several old stories told to her, anyone using a handbook like Belinda's when they weren't actually a fairy godmother usually suffered horrible results. Either by hurting themselves or by suffering the wrath of the Guild itself.

But trying to impart this bit of knowledge to the Ice Queen was more likely to incense the woman and make her think that Charlotte was trying to terrify her out of using the handbook or even trying to control or manipulate her.

In the fairy godmother's experience, villains rarely reacted well to being told what to do. When being warned about the use of something potentially dangerous, most of them were far more likely to do the dangerous thing anyway to try to prove them wrong rather than heed caution and listen to reason.

When Celeste still hadn't offered a response or done much besides glare spitefully at the fairy godmother and occasionally shoot a wary glance toward Cat, Charlotte's patience ran out. She could no longer wait without attempting to guide or push the sorceress in a different direction. Sometimes, a good push was necessary to get the ball rolling.

"Well?" Charlotte prompted, raising her eyebrows but keeping her wand steady. "Normally, I would be more than happy to let you take your time with something like this." She darted a glance around the enormous chamber. "But something tells me we don't have a lot of time here. I'm pretty sure the same thing applies to this entire quest cave after whatever you've done to it. So, unfortunately, I need you to make your decision. Now, if you don't mind."

The Ice Queen's sneer renewed with bitter vitriol before she spoke. "Just another one of those things they taught you in that infernal place they call a fairy godmother academy, huh? That the best way to get someone on your side is to use your manners. To act like you give a damn about what anyone else around you thinks or feels—"

"I *do* give a damn!" Charlotte shouted, her brows drawn. "You *don't* understand. Right now, I care quite a bit about what happens to you, my friend over here, and myself. I care about a great number of things, Celeste, which is why I'm trying to help you. This is a one-time offer, by the way. This won't last forever if you can't make up your mind."

In the interest of time and not wanting to take any more risk than she already had, Charlotte extended her free hand toward the Ice Queen, hoping the other woman would see the gesture as a sign of a temporary truce and tentative alliance. The safety of everyone in the chamber depended on it. Whatever ritual spell the witch had started, it wasn't over, and Charlotte didn't want to tempt Fate by letting this drag on longer than necessary.

A calculated risk was better than a reckless decision filled with uncontrollable variables. She could control this one courageous and admittedly overly optimistic effort to cease the fighting and start working with the villains wherever possible. Just like she had stopped following all her fairy godmother's training with Ginger Haus and took the time to listen to another supposed villain before making another snap judgment based on misconceptions that had piled up throughout Charlotte Weaver's fairy godmother career.

"What you don't understand is that I think we have more in common than you realize. So how about it then, huh?" Charlotte asked, widening her eyes and nodding as she extended her free hand a bit farther toward the Ice Queen, who was propped up on the ground, all the while maintaining her aim with the tip of her wand mere feet from the sorceress's face.

Celeste looked Charlotte up and down, multiple veins of thought and opposing emotions battling across her expression. "You would actually offer me this truce? In good faith and without trying to pull any other tricks?"

Charlotte sighed with relief she knew she probably shouldn't have felt yet, allowing it to show in her expression to encourage Celeste to take the offer hopefully.

"I would," Charlotte instantly replied. "I am. This is a real offer. Right here, right now. With no strings attached. Minus some ground rules, but we can cover that later. I promise you this isn't a trick, and while I don't particularly trust you, I do trust that you're smart enough to know when a good offer comes your way and when it's in your best interest to take it."

The Ice Queen's eyes widened before a short, airy chuckle escaped her. "Then you're a fool. No wonder you found yourself in Cincinnati with the rest of us."

Charlotte was taken aback. Her brows knit together in confusion. "What's that supposed to mean?"

"What do you *think* it means? The Guild got rid of you just like the rest of us!"

Despite her best efforts to remain firm in her conviction and her offer of truce and alliance with the sorceress who had gone from Prince Repel's partner in magical crime to a solo act seeking revenge on any number of EverAfterans and humans she felt had wronged her, the other woman's last statement had caught Charlotte completely off guard.

The few seconds of shocked silence that followed felt like they lasted forever before she finally responded. "What are you trying to say? I wasn't banished here on purpose. Not like you. Me being swept away into Cincinnati was an accident. Just a random fluke."

The Ice Queen snickered and shook her head, but something like pity crossed her face. "Then you haven't learned a damn thing, which means you can't do anything to help me."

A blast of cold air and frost exploded around the Ice Queen, forcing Charlotte and Cat to divert their eyes and shield their faces. When the fairy godmother's look darted back to where Celeste was just sitting, she found the spot bare and the frost dissipating.

Charlotte stood and stared in stunned silence. Her opponent had gotten away. *I lost her*, she thought.

And as her mind wandered back to everything that was just said, an icy chill that had nothing to do with the Ice Queen snaked its way down her spine.

Did the Guild banish me here...on purpose?

THE STORY CONTINUES

The story continues with book seven, *Spells, Wishes, and Retribution*, coming soon to Amazon and Kindle Unlimited.

Get sneak peeks, exclusive giveaways, behind the scenes content, and more. PLUS you'll be notified of special **one day only fan pricing** on new releases.

Sign up today to get free stories.

AUTHOR NOTES: MARTHA CARR

JUNE 24, 2024

I've started a project answering questions for my son about my life. I realized after the most recent fifth round of cancer, and then chemo this time, that he was expecting me to die sooner rather than later. It's been a lot for him to deal with and there isn't much I can do to make it better, except tell him stories that I can leave behind – eventually. Hopefully, a long time from now. I'm going to let you guys listen in as well.

My author notes right now are going to be answers to questions and all of you can get to know me better, too. Maybe inspire, maybe give you a laugh along the way.

Today's question is: What are some of your special talents?

I suppose there are three answers to this question. One would be the talents I was born with and didn't have to do much to really get the benefit from them. The next would be a combination of something I was born with mixed with a learned response that grew into something I could use. The last would be the skills I chose to cultivate and through hard work and a strong stubborn streak I made them into talents.

Let's go with the first one, first. I have the ability to see words in a pile of letters that are crammed together at a very fast rate. In college, I majored in psychology and was aware of all the psych tests going on that paid a little money. One of them was on word recognition and I scored abnormally high. It was not a surprise to me. Whereas I can't see numbers very well, ever, I can spot word groupings even in long, unending strings and discern meaning in seconds. My brain is always searching for those patterns.

Then there's that mixture of nature versus nurture. I grew up in a chaotic household and can be a little hyper-vigilant, (very much a learned response), assessing the moods of rooms very quickly and where everything is placed in case a hasty exit will be needed. This may have enhanced a skill I already had and made it better. I'm aware of body language, dialogue, mood and a hundred other small factors and therefore when I'm writing, I am also aware of the need to add it all in to make a fuller picture.

Then there's that last one where I chose to put in those 10,000 hours and seek out guidance and take the advice and make myself into a better writer. This is where being a staff writer and then a stringer for a major newspaper and then a columnist with a daily deadline made me into a much better fiction writer. All that daily practice with expectations from editors about style and length and telling a story succinctly with all the facts in a way that would make a reader want to read it and come back for more. Sound familiar?

For me, this somehow added up to becoming an author.

It started with that ability to form words and growing up in a household without a lot of extra money. Reading books from the library was one of the forms of entertainment I could count on that could take me anywhere. It wasn't like going somewhere with other kids where I knew our funds were limited and I might be standing on the sidelines from time to time, watching and wishing I could join in more. In a library I was on an equal footing and the same rules applied to all of us. On top of that, I could go find my own adventures to anywhere and the supply was unlimited. It opened up my world and gave me hope and inspiration about the future, and compassion and at least a little understanding about other people, other cultures.

That second one about the place where I grew up had just as much to do with funneling me toward being a writer. Not only did I learn to notice detail fast and well, I didn't say a whole lot. It was easier to be quiet and stick to the background. Hopefully, just fade away. But inside I had a voice that was dying to be heard and no outlet.

Until I started to write. That's where journalism and newspapers became so important for me. As a young adult I jumped over figuring out how to talk to the people right around me and started talking to the world in a place where no one was reframing my words as they came out of my mouth. It was liberating and the first time in my life I remember really being seen, heard, acknowledged and appreciated. That's an intoxicating elixir if you've never had it as a kid.

Of course I plowed ahead, determined to find my way

as a writer. It just hadn't occurred to me, at least yet, that I could figure out a way to be just as seen and just as heard among the people right around me. That would come later when I would figure out I needed to move far away and create a new community around me.

In the meantime, I took in every piece of advice and wrote and wrote and wrote. I was fortunate that my early editors were from the Washington Post and hammered into me how to write a really good, captivating sentence. Along with how to research an idea. It's not Google by the way.

Fortunately, over the years and lots of therapy I actually did learn how to speak up with those right around me. It also made it possible for them to really get to know me. I think I made it really hard for so many years that the best glimpse you could get of me was through my writing. It's also why I could never somehow motivate to go get a 'regular' job even when that was in my best interests. Going back to a weird kind of perfect silence would have overwhelmed me and been too much to bear.

I stuck it out and that talent I was born with, that was molded first by negative circumstances and then deliberately as I built my own rocket ship out of that place, became a pretty good writer of mostly magic running around Austin, Texas. It just keeps getting better. Love you. Love, Mom. More adventures to follow.

AUTHOR NOTES: MICHAEL ANDERLE

JUNE 18, 2024

First, thank you for not only reading this story, but these author notes in the back as well!

Las Vegas Eats: A Culinary Adventure

You know, one of the things I promised in another book was to share some of the delicious escapades I embark on here in Las Vegas. Let's be honest, this city is a smorgasbord of culinary delights, and every now and then, I like to play food critic.

So, here is the first time I've followed up ;-)

Yesterday, I had the pleasure of catching up with Charles Gerth, one of the fantastic folks who helps keep the gears turning at our company. Charles was staying at the Mirage Hotel for an Event for another one of his clients but didn't have to 'be there' until this morning. So I swung by to pick him up around 12:30 PM for lunch.

Now, Charles once treated Judith and I to some top-notch Chinese food in New York City, so I figured it was high time I returned the favor here in Vegas.

Enter China Mama 2. Yes, that's the spot I decided to take Charles for our little lunch outing. If you're ever in the mood for some amaze-balls Chinese cuisine, this place is a must-visit in my very humble opinion.

Stop laughing Martha – I am f@#$@%ing humble!

Here's the URL if you want to check it out: (https:// chinamama2.com/

As we dug into our feast, Charles and I got to reminiscing about some of our favorite meals from around the world. It's funny how food has a way of bringing people together, sparking memories, and creating new ones. We laughed, we strategized, and we might have even indulged in a bit of people-watching.

(We were the only two (2) white-guys in the restaurant. I did mention we were in China town, right?)

But beyond the great food and company, what really struck me was the realization of how far we've come. From humble beginnings to enjoying a fantastic meal in one of the most vibrant cities on the planet, it's been quite the journey. And it's moments like these that remind me of the importance of taking a step back, savoring the little things, and appreciating the readers who make life's journey so worthwhile.

So, if you ever find yourself in Las Vegas, do yourself a favor and swing by China Mama 2. Trust me, your taste buds will thank you. And who knows, maybe you'll create some unforgettable memories of your own.

Until the next adventure, keep exploring, keep enjoying, and keep savoring every moment

Ad Aeternitatem,
Michael Anderle

P.S. If you enjoyed this story, please take a moment to leave a review. Your kind words and encouragement mean the world to me. And don't forget to subscribe to the MORE STORIES with Michael newsletter HERE: https://michael.beehiiv.com/

BOOKS BY MARTHA CARR

Other Series in the Oriceran Universe:

JOIN THE ORICERAN UNIVERSE FAN GROUP ON FACEBOOK!

CONNECT WITH THE AUTHORS

Martha Carr Social

Website: http://www.marthacarr.com

Facebook: https://www.facebook.com/groups/
MarthaCarrFans/

Michael Anderle Social

Website: http://lmbpn.com

Email List: https://michael.beehiiv.com/

https://www.facebook.com/LMBPNPublishing

https://twitter.com/MichaelAnderle

https://www.instagram.com/lmbpn_publishing/

https://www.bookbub.com/authors/michael-anderle